I0692002

The Four B's:

Big, Bold, Black and Beautiful

First Edition

Published by the Nazca Plains Corporation
Las Vegas, Nevada
2014

ISBN: 978-1-61098-375-4
E-Book: 978-1-61098-376-1

Published by
The Nazca Plains Corporation®
4640 Paradise Rd, Suite 141
Las Vegas, NV 89109-8000

PUBLISHER'S NOTE
The Four B's: Big, Bold, Black and Beautiful is a work of fiction created
wholly by Wade Wright's imagination. All characters are fictional and
any resemblance to any persons living or deceased is purely by accident.
No portion of this book reflects any real person or events.

Cover Photo, Stockyimages
Art Director, Blake Stephens

To every Big, Bold, Black and Beautiful gay
man that is out there. Do please enjoy life,
and do help others enjoy life, with you.

The Four B's:

Big, Bold, Black and Beautiful

First Edition

Wade Wright

Contents

At the Hawaiian Bed and Breakfast

It was heaven, unadulterated, blissful heaven! The smells of the flora, the fauna, the soft ocean breezes, and of course the beautiful scent of the ocean air – it was, and is, all unadulterated – blissful – heaven!

I'm from the southwestern desert, and I love the desert, but there is no way to imagine that the smells and the sensations of the shores of the big island of Hawaii can be beat by any other place or location.

Jean and I were visiting, for five days, at what we simply call, "Bob and Sandi's house," on the shoreline close to Hilo, on the big island. Bob and Sandi are just short of retirement age, and for about twenty years now, have owned and run this beautiful retreat of heaven, for some of the most fortunate individuals that have ever visited the tropics of Hawaii. The actual house is very Hawaiian in character and style, and can accommodate up to five couples at a time, in some of the most beautiful and delightful room accommodations that any person could hope for or desire.

About two years ago, Jean and I had happened to discover this rather private and hidden oasis of a tropical environment when we were on a self-guided sightseeing tour of the eastern side of the island. On that particular night, Bob and Sandi absolutely insisted that we stay long enough to have dinner with them and the houseguests. It was during that short, but very delicious visit that we promised ourselves, and Bob and Sandi, that we would be back for a much longer visit, sometime within the next two years. The time had now come! We were there! And everything was even more beautiful and smelled even better than we remembered from our first visit.

During this visit, the house was full. One couple, Shawn and Carol were young, in their early twenties and were on their honeymoon. The second couple were nice folks, but not really the conversation type. From New Jersey and probably in their mid to later sixty's. They obviously did prefer to live a much more quiet and private life, and we allowed them that comfort. The third couple was Tyron and Brian. A gay couple that we found out had been together for more than fifteen or sixteen years. Both men were office managers for a large Minnesota company. They were delightful to be around and to talk to. They were full of helpful information about all of the islands of Hawaii! Once a year, they visited a different place on the islands, and this year it was Bob and Sandi's.

Couple number four was Jean and I, the mid thirty's couple that did come from the desert, as I had mentioned, and were celebrating a full week of vacation away from the thirteen and the fifteen year olds. Love 'em dearly, but a week in the tropics without them has its major values also!

Now the fifth couple, they were the really fun ones for Jean and I to get to know. Chase and Nancy.

Chase, as we found out, was a printing foreman for a large printing company close to St. Louis, and about a year earlier his company had printed a magazine that included an article that mentioned Bob and Sandi's bed and breakfast. Chase took a copy of the article home and told Nancy, "That is where we are gonna be for our fifteenth anniversary!"

I will admit that when we met Chase and Nancy, and he told us that he was a printing foreman, I guess my mouth rather dropped, or at least I looked kinda shocked. Chase looked at me and asked why I had such a shocked expression. Feeling kinda stupid and maybe embarrassed some, I finally did get it out, that for the body he was carrying around, I certainly did rather expect him to say he was something like a professional wrestler. Stood about six foot two or three, looked to weigh in at about two hundred and maybe fifteen or twenty, a chest on him that any large shirt would have problems covering, and a waist that could easily use only a thirty three or thirty four inch belt.

Me, I'm in construction, but sure not carrying around the type of body that man is! I'm almost sure that if our construction company could hire that man for on the team, we'd get more work, just so the customers could hire us and watch him work. Stunning! His mahogany toned skin and his slick shaved head, sitting above that, probably, eighteen/nineteen inch thick neck, obviously added to his stunning appearance.

We arrived at Bob and Sandi's on Sunday afternoon, and Chase and Nancy arrived shortly afterwards. All of the other guests had arrived on Saturday. Maybe our arriving close together created the early and easy bond between the four of us – Jean and I and Chase and Nancy.

Sunday evening was sheer delight, and the cooking that Sandi did certainly did add to that delight, and to the aromas that we were taking in deeply with total pleasures! Since Chase and

Nancy, and I and Jean are pretty close to the same age, and of course having children about the same age, made it very easy to get to know each other, and to share living and life experiences, back on the 'mainland.'

Sunday and Monday were the great typical vacation days, well if you can call a visit to the Hawaiian Islands anything close to typical! It was on Tuesday morning that we, Jean and I, and Chase and Nancy decided to take advantage of one of the rather private beachside lounging areas and just do a kickback afternoon of sipping some good liquid stuff, okay – cocktails, and having some good conversation.

Sandi fixed us a good supply of liquids and a picnic basket full of snacks and goodies of all sorts, and then set us out to enjoy the Hawaiian beach, air breezes and the flora and fauna. We were in heaven! Unadulterated – blissful – heaven!

As we wound our way through the tropical forest, a light forest yes, but nonetheless, to us mainlanders – a forest, we discovered that Bob had already visited the site and had prepared it with cushions, beach mats, shade umbrellas, and some additional liquid enjoyments for us to enjoy.

The ladies rather continued their previous conversations about, the children, the groceries, the PTA meetings, the soccer games, the long telephone conversations, the traffic jams, the cooking, the laundry and just about every other item that two women could think about. They each sounded as if they never had anybody close to them to discuss all of these important items.

The conversation between Chase and I was much more calm, and restrained. We discussed business matters, his printing profession, my construction profession, the weather, the flights over to the islands, some politics and of course other little items that just might happen to enter into the topic of the moment.

Without saying it, it was pretty damned obvious to anybody, that with the body that Chase was carrying around, he looked pretty damn good sitting out there, "getting a suntan" in the tight, form fitting, butt hugging, and crotch grabbing square cut bottom trunks that he had on. I will admit that once or twice, as I looked over at him, that I was amazed that neither Tyron nor Brian had kidnapped him and taken him off into the tropics for one hell of a hot time! I had never thought of two men attempting to take advantage of one man in that fashion before, but on this day, I did! Even for me, the straight daddy guy that had never lusted over anything except a female, it was pretty damn hard to keep from looking at the package he carried in those shorts! With a body like that, all of the parts, even the hidden parts, had to be pretty damn good looking.

I was lounging on a lounge chair, and Chase had seated himself on a beach mat, with his legs crossed much the same way that we see pictures and drawings of the native Indians sitting around a fire. That position definitely spread his legs wide, and presented one very bulging crotch area for full view! It did look like it did have an Idaho potato stuffed in there! And a big one at that!

I guess maybe Chase did catch me, unconsciously, looking down toward his crotch – which was in full display, and facing directly toward me, and then quickly trying to stop what I was obviously doing, and should not be doing. As I rather jerked my head back up and into its proper position, I'd see him grinning rather widely at me. This did not happen only once, but probably three or four times. I do remember that during the second or third time, as he grinned, he then looked down at my crotch, and grinned again, and then looked up at my face. I was trying hard to maintain my composure and dignity and not act as if I had noticed or seen anything unusual happening. I quickly restarted our subject of conversation, and I will admit I did hope I was back on the same subject that we had been discussing. Once or twice, I was not so sure I was! My checking out his crotch was certainly not normal for me. I had never checked out some other guy's crotch before, and the fact that I was checking out his, was really confusing me! Why? Why was I doing this?

Suddenly and without warning, Chase asked, "Hey Ben, wanna go for a walk and see what's around the big point?"

Kinda shocked and surprised at the question, I quickly said, "Yeah, yeah. You wanna?"

"Yeah let's do! I don't think it's too far of a walk, and from what Bob said last night, the only way so get there is to walk the beach since there's no roads over there. I'd kinda like to see what's there."

Then looking at his wife and Jean, he asked, "Hey ladies, that okay if Ben and I take a hike? You two are really talking all that lady stuff and don't even know we're here, so okay if we do?"

As both of the women gave their approval of the actions, Chase and I did get up, put our beach shoes on, and told the ladies that since we did not know for sure just how long we would be gone, and if they went back to the house before we got back, just load up all of our stuff, and we'd see 'em at the house. We then took off down the beach.

The 'big point,' as it's referred to, is where the island juts out into the ocean some, and obviously does have a good view of the beach area on both sides of it.

As Chase and I walked, we talked – small talk, just like back at the lounge area, but as we did, I'd often notice Chase stop, bend over, his ass toward me, and then pick up some small item and look at it, like perhaps maybe a seashell. Yes, I saw his ass! One nice looking ass for somebody that did not maybe own a gym! Once he stopped, bent over right in front of me and picked up something to look at, and for a slight moment I did – I know I did – I saw him looking at my crotch from only about ten or twelve inches away. Never had I ever had a man's face that close to my crotch, and yes, I admit it, it rather made me excited. As he stood back up, he looked at me directly in the face and grinned. I smiled back. What else was I supposed to do? Maybe I've never had a man that close to my crotch before, but I sure as hell was not gonna get mad at this guy – the size of him and the muscles on him? And besides, I knew for some funny reason it was kinda of exciting to me, so why should I act like I was pissed? Maybe my grin or my smile back to him was a little more natural and honest than I really thought it should be.

As we walked and talked, we did obviously keep a good keen eye on the beautiful ocean and tropical views that were presented before us. The ocean and the slight ocean waves sweeping up toward us was a true treat. The desert did not have this type of beauty nor did the St. Louis area. If we stood still and silent, the quietness of the area, and then the ocean and water sounds were a total treat! This was a tropical heaven!

As we walked, suddenly Chase turned, and headed into the tropical growth and slightly away from the beach. He turned to look back to see if I was following. I did. Not too sure of just the what, and the why, we were moving back into some of the tropical growth, but I did follow. After about three or four minutes of walking into some deeper and deeper growth, Chase stopped, turned, looked at me and asked, "Okay, whose first?"

"First!? First what!?" I rather emphatically asked, as I looked into one very handsome face that I had been admiring all day.

As Chase grabbed onto his crotch, he tugged at it, and then said, "I wanna suck on you, and I'm hoping you wanna suck on me!"

"Oh my gawd man! Chase, you what!?" I was stunned! Shocked, and stunned! I had been seeing him rather eye balling me, but I sure as hell never thought about anything like this happening!

With one swift move, Chase moved his hand from the outside of his crotch and in a split second, he had dropped his trunks down and displayed one of the biggest and of course darkest dicks that I had ever seen. I had never been around any black men in a shower room. My whole school was white guys. So this big thick stiff black dick was a totally new experience for me. And it was hard! Very hard! And as it stood there, it kept getting harder and harder! I could tell! It was obvious! It was growing!

"See man, I've got a hard-on, and I need to feel you grabbing onto it! Come on Ben, do it! I wanna feel you doing it! I wanna feel your hand on it and rubbing it! I gotta know, when I get back home, that I had some good fucking fun out here beside the ocean getting my dick played with! I've never done anything like this outdoors before, and man, out here I need it! I do! This air has got me all turned on man! Come on man, help me out here! I saw you checking out my basket earlier. You looked at it, I know you did."

Totally stunned, and I do mean totally stunned, I stood there and looked at the biggest dick I had ever seen on a man – or in some funny magazine that one of my friends had when I was a kid. It was enormous! Yes, yes I will admit, I wanted to touch it. I could not believe Chase actually had his dick out and was begging for me to do something to it!

"It's okay man, it's okay! Come on! Make my day for me! Let me feel you grab onto it! Help me do something really exciting here man, help me!"

Now looking up at him, and then down at it, I really was confused as to just what I was doing. I kept telling myself, 'No man, no! You can't do that! That's not right,' and at the same time, I was telling myself, 'Do it man, do it! Look at it! Look how fucking big it is! When are you ever gonna get to do this again? Do it, do it!'

I guess my 'Do it,' won out! Without really even thinking about what I was doing, I reached out and put my hand around it, well as much as I could! It was warm! It was stiff – stiff as a piece of steel, and it made my heart beat like it was gonna fall apart! I had never taken another man's dick in my hand! All of a sudden, as I was feeling it, and actually for just how long I had it in my hand I did not know – since I felt like I was totally unconscious as to just what I was doing – I felt Chase slide his fingers into the top of my Speedos and slide 'em down. All of a sudden I could feel the cool moist air hitting my dick, and even though it was already hard, it got harder! The cool moist ocean air even blew up in my butt, which made me that much more excited! Now both of us were there with our dicks sticking out and having a hand from the other man, grabbing onto it.

"Rub it man, come on man, rub my dick!"

Looking up at Chase, all I could see was his expression of hope and pleasure at the idea that I had my hand on his dick, and out there in the great tropical out of doors, right beside the ocean, maybe he was gonna get some treatment that he could only hope for.

"Rub it man, please, please! Come on Ben, rub it and lick on it! Please! Please! Lick it man, lick it! Please!"

Without any thought process in my mind at all, I simply obeyed his rather direct orders of, "Lick it man, lick it!" and I did! Never before in my entire life had I ever even thought about licking on some man's dick, but right then I was totally taken over and controlled by this 'man' that all I could think of was, he was more than just man! I stooped down, opened my mouth and for the very first time in my life, I fed my mouth onto the head of a man's cock! I reached around and grabbed his ass! I grabbed tight and I pulled tight! I took him into my mouth as fast as I could, but choked almost immediately! He was big! Damn big! My mouth was full and I was still trying to take more and more of him and 'it!' I knew that if I spread my thumb and fingers apart, from tip to tip, that was nine inches. This was just part of being in the construction business. In that business, you learn funny things like that! Well, thumb and fingers spread as far as possible, and now resting up against his enormous beautiful dark mahogany cock, even with the head of his dick stuck in my mouth, my finger and thumb did not reach end to end! The part of his dick, still not in my mouth, was more than nine inches! Never, in my entire life, had I even so much as grabbed onto another guy's dick, and now here I was, on vacation in Hawaii with my wife, and now out in the beautiful tropical growth, beside the Pacific Ocean, and I was eating as much, as humanly possible, of the biggest, hottest, stiffest, thickest dick, that was probably on any of the islands! It was great, and even though I knew in my mind, that was something I was not supposed to be doing – I was doing it – and I was enjoying it! This big, tremendous hunk of a man that was standing there, right in front of my face, had told me to do it – and I did!

Chase grabbed onto my head and pumped his dick, good and hard with my head! I groaned and I grunted, but I never tried to tell him to stop! I grabbed onto his ass muscles – much tighter! I was turned on! Never had I ever thought I'd ever do anything like this, but I was totally out of control! I pushed my face into him that much stronger! I sucked on him as hard as I could! I buried my face in his crotch as close as I could since he had way,

way, too much cock for me to swallow all of it! For four or five minutes, I sucked and I chewed and I made mad passionate love to that dick! I loved it. All of it! The entire dick and all of its flavor!

All of a sudden I heard Chase let out with, "Oh my gawd man, oh Ben – I'm gonnnnnna – Ben – I'm gonnnna cummm man – I'm gonnnna!"

I wanted to watch his cum fly, and I pulled off just as he let out about three times with, "Oh shit man – oh shit! Oh fuck, that feels so fucking good! Oh man, what a hit! Oh Ben! What a feeling man – what a feeling! Oh thanks man, thanks!"

I scooted back just far enough when he started to let it all fly, that I actually watched probably a half cup of cum, come flying out of his enormous dick. I had cum all over my chest, my neck, my arms, my face and my hands! I was covered!

"Oh man! Oh Ben, you're a mess! Ben – you've got cum all over you! Oh shit man, look at how much I shot off on you! Shit man, you're a mess!"

"Chase, I know I'm a mess! I can see that! But what's more important to me right now is that I'm about as horny as I've ever been in my entire life, and I need to get sucked off, now! You game, or you just a giver? Will you suck me off, please!?"

Without saying anything, Chase stooped over, grabbed me under the arms, stood me up, then stooped down and showed me how a real man sucks a cock.

"Oh shit man! My cock sure isn't the first cock you've sucked on is it! Damn man, do it, do it! I've never had a man sucking on me, so make damn sure you do it so that I never forget this vacation! Yeah man, yeah! Oh my gawd man! Oh Chase, I'm gonna cum man, I'm gonna cum!"

Grabbing me tighter and tighter, pulling me in closer and closer, and of course being able to take all of my dick like he did, just as he opened his mouth and went down on it, I heard Chase grunt an, "Okay, okay!" I had never shot off my dick juices in anybody's mouth before, and when it started flying, I had already heard Chase grunt the "Okay," so I grabbed ahold of the back of his head, and I fed him all that I had! I pulled his face forward, and he pulled my ass toward him too. He ate everything I had to offer! He pulled off my dick, kissed the end of it, licked the end of it, looked up at me, and asked, "Hey guy! I wanna take another hike tomorrow! You interested!?"

Right then all I could say was, "As long as your dick don't get no bigger than it did today! I wanna take the hike, but I sure can't take any more dick than you fed me today! You sure did something to me today that I never thought I'd ever be doing! What a way to remember my time out by the beautiful Pacific! Come on, I need to take a short swim and kinda clean myself up some before we head back to the wives! Thank God your anniversary is this week."

"Ben, without this happening, I'm afraid this whole trip would have just been another anniversary, but with you sucking on my dick, and you letting me suck you off for your first time, I will never forget this anniversary. Tomorrow is the true anniversary, and tomorrow I am gonna do you, and let you do me, so that I really have one great anniversary to remember!"

As we headed down the beach and back into our secret "sex playing space the next day, I told Chase, "Oh Chase, I really cannot believe this! I know damned well Jean and Nancy had other ideas of what they wanted to do this afternoon, but your suggestion that they go do some Hawaiian shopping today, sure was a brilliant move. I know we did some stuff yesterday out here, but man, I gotta admit that I think I'm more nervous today than I was then. Seriously man, all yesterday afternoon – after we got back to the house – and then yesterday evening and today too, I have never been so excited about doing something that I know us guys are not supposed to be doing, but still, looking forward to it so much. You know – my entire life I've been told by everybody, including some ministers – ministers that probably do each other – that men are really sick if they do this stuff together, but if so, right now the medicine I need for my sickness is your rod! Chase, you know damn well that yesterday was my first time doing something with a guy, and I gotta tell you man, what a guy I got to do it with – and for my first time! Chase, do you know other guys that are hung as big as you are? Have you ever played around with some guy that is hung that big?"

"Oh yeah Ben, I'm not the biggest dick out there. I know, my dick is big, but believe me, I've played with bigger ones!"

As we headed back into the native cover a little farther than we had been the day before, I asked Chase, "What in the hell did you do with him? I mean, if his dick was larger than yours, what in the hell could you do with it? Just rub it or jack it off?"

Looking over at me, Chase grinned and told me, "Oh no man, not just rub it or jack it off! It was definitely much more like, suck it off, and then get fucked in the ass with it!"

I sprung my head over at Chase, to the point I damn near fell face first into the sand, and almost screamed, "Got fucked by it!!? How in the hell can a guy get fucked in the ass with something that fucking big? Chase, you just told me his was bigger than yours! Come on man, there is no way in hell that you could have gotten fucked by something that fucking big! Right? You really didn't get fucked, did you?"

"Yeah, I did! And I will admit, the first fucking that I got was with the biggest dick I have ever been fucked by. Some of the others have been big, but Bro Bubby's was the biggest?"

"Bro Bubby? Who in the hell was Bro Bubby, and first, why do you know his name, who was he, and did you really get

fucked by this Bro Bubby? Come on man, you gotta fill me in.
I've never talked to some guy that admits he's been fucked in the
ass before, so now you've got me so fucking hot listening to this
stuff, you gotta tell me! I've got a bunch of construction workers
around me all of the time, and I thought once I might of overheard
one guy telling another guy something about getting it up in the
ass the night before, but of course I never mentioned it, but I will
admit, I've wondered ever since then, if that is what could have
happened. Come on man, now's the time to fill me in and let me
learn some stuff that I probably should already know. Chase,
what happened the first time? How did he get to you? What
happened?"

"It was about twelve years ago. I was like twenty-three at
the time. I was at a printing convention in Chicago. Bunch of us
were drinking at some bar down the street from the hotel, and I
got to talking to some guy – Bro Bubby as it turns out – and while
we were still there at the bar, he kept feeding me shots and more
shots, and then really got to talking about my chest. One thing
led to another, to where he told me he wanted to see me without
a shirt on, and I will admit, I was starting to wonder about him
without a shirt on too. He was a really good looking man, and
was one hell of a built guy."

"Was he one of the guys from the convention? Was he
someone that you already knew?"

"No, no! He was just a guy there at the bar, and he sat
down on a stool beside me, and then a little later, after we talked
for a while, he suggested that we move over to a counter area that
was a little more out of the way, and that's when he really started
talking about my chest, and yes – once did lay his hand down on
my crotch! By that time, he had fed me enough shots, that I didn't
move it or tell him to take it off! It felt good there. Kinda felt
like I had a puppy lying there making my crotch warm. The other

guys from the convention that I had gone to the bar with, came by our area and told me that they were gonna head back to the hotel, and I told 'em that I'd be there in a little while. That's when Bro Bubby started suggesting that we go over to his apartment so we could look at each other's chests without shirts on. At first, I kinda said, 'No,' but I guess not very convincingly! He laid his hand down on my leg and then kinda moved it over toward my crotch a little, and kept asking me if I would. He told me he had some more stuff to drink over at the apartment, and he kept telling me how he just wanted to see my chest. That was gonna be all. He just wanted to see my chest bare, and then maybe compare it to his, to see who had the nicest looking chest."

"You call him Bro, does that mean he's a black man too?"

"Oh yeah! Yeah black, and I mean black! A lot darker than me. Darker than me, and hung about twice as long as me! Hot as hell! Body to fucking die for!"

"Oh shit man, I have never been this fucking hot just listening to some guy talk about some other guy! Chase, you have got me so fucking turned on listening about you and this Bro guy, I am about to shoot some cum without even touching my dick. I have to assume you did go home with him, right?"

"Oh yeah! Yeah, I sure did! There at the bar he kept telling me that his place was only about a four minute walk from the bar, and he really wanted me to come over, 'for a few minutes!' Oh yeah! A few minutes my eye! It was more like about three hours! But God those were three hot hours! I got fucked that night! Not only did I get fucked, but I fucked his hot ass too!"

"Oh shit man, oh God Chase, I am getting fucking weak in the knees! We better get to wherever we're gonna stop, cause you are telling me stuff that I have never heard from any other guy before, and I guess maybe I'm in the mood for it – or it's just that you are such, one hot looking guy, and I already know what you are hanging down there between your legs – that now – I am looking at some stuff in a totally new and different way! What in the hell happened then!? God, tell me man! Shit! I never expected this afternoon to turn out anything like this!"

"I finally agreed to go to his place, but just to take our shirts off and look at each other's chest, and that was all! He agreed. We talked while we walked over to his place, and he told me, 'Well, you think I've got a nice looking chest now – just you wait until I can get this shirt off and some other stuff, and then I'll show you the part I'm most proud of!'"

"I really did not completely comprehend or catch on to what he was really saying about 'some other stuff.' Gotta remember, I'd been drinking some pretty hot shots for about two hours before this, so I really was not in the clearest of minds."

"Within just a couple of minutes, we had reached Bro Bubby's front door, and as we entered, Bro asked me, 'Hey, want something to drink? I've got some Bud in the frig if you want.'"

"I accepted the offer, and with Bro's instruction, I did go to the kitchen and got two Buds from the refrigerator. Bro Bubby then excused himself and went into the bedroom."

"I was seated at the dining room table when Bro came back out from the bedroom, fully and completely naked and hot as hell! He took off one hell of a lot more than just his shirt! I was shocked way beyond belief, when he walked in! Bro's dark brown, highly toned body, all of the muscles in his chest, his arms, his legs and of course, his butt were absolutely beautiful, beautiful and outstanding! His chest tapered down to a waist line that I felt like I could simply put my hands around, and the washboard stomach was enough to make me wanna wash clothes and then use it as a real washboard!"

"I admit I almost screamed, 'Oh my God! Oh shit man – you look good! Oh Bro, I sure as hell never expected you to just

come out here all naked and bare assed like that! Oh shit man!
I'm not used to guys just walking around all naked and bare like
that! Oh man, you got one hell of a hot looking body! Shit man!
I used to wrestle in high school, and I thought I'd wrestled some
pretty well built guys in the past, but fuck man – nothing that
looks like you! Oh shit man, you are hot!'"

"Then I realized that I was actually looking at his dick! I
did not think going over to his place was gonna turn out anything
like this! There I was, a straight married guy, sitting there and
only about two feet away was the longest, thickest, strongest,
darkest stick of meat that I had ever seen, in a magazine or even
in the sausage section of the meat counter! I told him, 'Oh my
god man – you have got the dick of death on you!' And then
I could not believe I actually asked him, 'How fucking long is
that thing?' I could not believe that I was actually asking some
other guy how big his dick was! I hadn't even asked some of my
buddies, when I was younger, how big their dicks were!"

"Then he told me, 'Well, to be honest, right now not as
long as it will be if I can get you to touch it! It's not hard yet!
Come on man, touch it and make it get really hard!'"

"We had gone over to his place just to be able to take our
shirts off and compare our chests, and now here he was standing
right in front of my face with the prettiest piece of meat hanging
there, begging to get touched and handled! I took one long deep
breath and not even realizing what in the hell I was doing, I picked
it up and licked the tip of it! That is when it did start getting hard!
And it kept getting hard! All of a sudden – and I do mean all of
a sudden – I was into some good hard, long, and stiff, gay sex. I
had never, ever wanted to touch some guy's dick, let alone put my
tongue on it, and here I was, I was holding it up to my face and I
was licking it! Three minutes earlier I would have told anybody,
that there was no way in hell that I would even touch some other

guy's cock, and now – here all of a sudden, I'm licking what looked like the biggest fudge sickle on the face of the earth.

I know I sure as hell was not thinking too good, but I was thinking well enough to know that I was being given the opportunity of a lifetime – with a dick hanging on the front of a man – that had the body – that was way, way, beyond belief!"

"Oh my God Chase! Chase you have gotten me so fucking hard, I cannot believe it! Oh shit man, I cannot believe this! I did not know until yesterday playing around with you then, and now you telling me about your Bro Bubby, that I guess really hot, big built guys do turn me on! Oh what in the hell did you do then?"

"I lost all control! Seriously man, I did! I had never in my entire life ever thought that I wanted to put the tip of some guy's dick in my mouth, and here I was, all of a sudden, eating every inch of that dick that I could push in my mouth. I started down on that dick, and then all of a sudden realized that he had what felt like two lemons in that fuzzy soft bag back behind his dick. I had never touched any other guy's bag or balls before, but all of a sudden, I fell in love with those two nuts. I will admit, until then, I never actually realized that guys sucked and chewed on other guys' balls, but I sure as hell went for the natural actions. Getting both of 'em in my mouth at the same time was a challenge, but I managed it, and I guess he loved it cause he kept moaning and groaning and telling me to, 'Keep it up man, keep it up!"

"Of course that was the first time I had done a lot of stuff, but of course, it was the first time that I had ever had some man grab ahold of the sides of my head, pull it into his crotch, and lock it there! I think I was wondering just what in the hell was I doing, but at the same time, I really did not care! I was way too fucking excited to be just making love to this man, to his tight, strong, skin, to all of the muscles on him, and of course to that enormous big, thick, stiff, dick of his. For some ole straight guy, I sure did go for all of the man stuff that he was letting me take. And I gotta admit, he wasn't 'making' me take it, he was 'letting' me take it, and I was going for it all with all the gusto I could manage! I had never, up until right at that time, ever played with some other guy's body, but I was then, and I was fucking enjoying it, and have never denied it!"

"He told me to put my hand back on his ass! I did! One small instruction from him, and I was doing it. I felt him reach over to the table, dip his finger in something, and then smear it up in his ass. Then he told me to put my finger up in there! I did! Like I said, one small instruction from him, and I was his obedient boy!"

"How old was this guy? You said you were his 'boy.' Was he older than you? Is that why you called yourself his boy?"

"No! No, not really! He was two years older than me, but he sure as hell looked like he had spent about twenty years more than me in the weight room! One unbelievable body on him! When I first met him in the bar, I really did not realize just how hot of a body he had! Well, guess maybe that's because until he came walking out of his bedroom all undressed and letting everything hang out, I had never, really ever, been that interested in checking out how some guy was built! Well, that little session sure did change all of that!"

"I was sitting there on the chair, he was standing in front of me, and I was putting my finger up in his ass! I was wiggling it around up in there! I had my finger in his ass! I could not believe it! I had never thought about wanting to put a finger up in some guy's ass! I had my face glued to his crotch and his dick, and now I had a finger going up in his ass! I was almost out of my mind realizing just what in the hell I was doing! All of a sudden, I was in fucking heaven! I was! I took my other hand and I reached around to his ass and I grabbed ahold of his butt cheek and pulled his crack apart and then put two, then three, more fingers up in his ass! I know, I remember – how like all of a sudden – I kinda came back to reality and fully understood that I was now making love, true love to one fucking hot built, muscled man, and I was kissing his dick, his fuzzy crotch and at the same time making love to his ass and feeling the insides of his ass – with my fingers! To this day, it still kinda shakes me to realize that I had actually put my fingers up inside of that guy's ass – that soon – after he came into the room all bare assed naked!"

"Oh Chase – Chase! I gotta stop here and get these trunks off! You have got me so fucking hot, I feel like I'm the one sitting there and getting to put my fingers up in his ass! Oh God, I hope you'll let me do that to you! Oh man, that is about the hottest thing I have ever thought about! I have never had any kind of a conversation like this with anyone! Honestly, right now I feel like I'm some young kid just now starting to find out what grown up people do."

Looking at me and then grinning widely, Chase then said, "I know, that's the way I felt that day too. He had really gotten me all hot and bothered! Yeah, fingers up in his ass was hot, but not as hot as when he told me he wanted my dick up in there! That is about when I fucking fainted. All of a sudden, all of my drinking and being about three fourth's drunk, totally went away! He reached around to his ass, pushed my hand up into his ass as much as he could, then pulled it out and reached around to me, and helped me stand up! From that point on, I did not even know really what was happening, or if it was real, or if it was make-believe! I was having troubles realizing that I was not drunk, I was not asleep, and I was really standing there and getting fully undressed, by the hottest looking man I that I had ever seen in any magazine, any gym or even any movie!"

"I had a pull-over shirt on, and he pulled that up and off of my head like he was unwrapping the most expensive present he had ever had! When it came off of my face, I thought I was looking at the most amazing bronze statue that had ever been cast. For just that half of a second that my eyes were under that shirt, I felt like it had been years since I had seen that sight! Just as soon as he pulled that shirt up and off of my wrists, so that my arms were free, I grabbed him by the sides of his face and planted the biggest and the longest kiss on him, and his lips, that I think any man has ever planted on any other man! That half of a second while I could not see him, I really think I got lonesome for him. He was that fucking hot to me."

"He threw my shirt off to the side, then he sat me back down and slowly and carefully took off my left shoe and sock, and then my right shoe and sock. He was kneeling down right in front of me, full bare body acting as if this was an everyday duty."

"He stood up, and of course that entire twelve inch dick pointed right at my face as he reached down and lifted me up, by grabbing ahold of me under my arm pits. When he stood up, I felt like I could look all the way up and inside of his whole body, by simply looking into what, I thought, was the most beautiful pee hole that could be on any living thing! I just thought, 'There is no wild animal, out in some wild jungle that could have a better, rounder, deeper pee hole than that one was!' Never, and I do mean never, had I ever thought about somebody else's pee hole, but all of a sudden, I wanted it made into a life sized stone monument! I guess maybe the pee hole, the dick it was in, and of course, also, the man that cock was attached to! Oh! If it could have been in black marble – oh that would have looked just like him! Oh the color would have been just right!"

"I stood there and watched him unbuckle my belt, unzip my pants and then put his fingers in the top of my briefs and slowly, lovingly, carefully slide them down and then immediately, and I do immediately, kiss my boner! It jumped and moved more with that kiss than it had ever done before! If my pee hole could have talked, I know damn well it would have yelled, "Suck me hot man, suck on me!"

"Did he!? Did he suck you?"

"Oh yes – oh yes he did!" As Chase stood there, turned his head up, closed his eyes and slowly shook his head up and down, he replied, "Oh yes he did. That was the very first time that I had felt a man's mouth, gift-wrap my dick, and he did it perfectly! Absolutely perfectly!"

"For probably ten or twelve minutes, he sucked on my dick like it was a twenty-four hour lollypop, and chewed on it like maybe it was the drumstick from a Thanksgiving Day turkey. And the more he chewed, the more I really wanted him to bite some of it off, so that he'd have part of me inside of him! He sucked on it once really very, very, hard and very strong, and then he grabbed some lube that was on the table, slid some of it up in his ass, laid down on the carpet, right here in the dining room, and told me to, 'Fuck me!' Nothing more! Just the simple, 'Fuck me!'"

"Seriously, he knew I had never fucked some guy before, but he sure as the hell never asked me if I wanted to or not, he just told me to fuck him! And like I said before, one small instruction from him, and I obeyed! I had never fucked some guy's ass before, but I sure as the hell was not gonna refuse this one!"

"I laid down on his ass, grabbed ahold of his butt cheek muscles, kinda spread 'em apart, and I almost felt like I fell in! I threw my face right down between his ass cheeks and I licked, and I licked like I had never licked anything in my entire life before! I had buried my face in his butt and I had driven my nose right up into his ass. I licked, and I bit on his butt, like I knew what in the hell I was doing. He had not even told me to put my face in there, nor had he told me to lick his ass, but for some unexplained natural reason, I did, as if I had to! No, I sure as hell did not have to, but if anybody had tried to pull my face away from that ass, I'm sure I would have slugged the hell out of 'em! Right then, that tight muscled dark ass was the hottest thing on the face of the earth, and right then, it was mine, and I was using it! I was eating it, and I was making true face, lip and ass action like had never been done before! Well, as far as I knew, nobody had ever eaten out an ass as hot as that one before! I had breakfast, lunch and dinner on that ass, and I even had some sweet sweat desert."

"I finally pulled my face back and off of it, I licked my lips dry, and I moved up on this magnificent body of a man, and I aimed my dick! Right as I felt the rim of his tight ass grab onto the tip of my dick, I pushed! He let out just a small, 'Oh,' and then pushed his ass up toward me, telling me, without saying anything, that I was in! I was in all the way, and now it was time to give his ass what it was asking for – one hell of a fucking – and in one hell of a big strong way!"

"I had never fucked a muscled butt before. I had never laid down on some guy's back and fucked his tight hole, but I sure did not need lessons to find out what to do! I fucked that hole, I grabbed on his body, I kissed his neck, I chewed on his ears, and I know damn well that when I came, I must have scratched the hell out of his arms! When I came, I damn near screamed in his ears! I had never, not even on our wedding night, ever shot a load as forcefully as I did into his butt that night! I shook the fucking floor with the pressure I loaded his ass with! Man, I had never had anything close to that experience happen to me before!"

"Ben, I know what you're about to ask! Yeah – yeah I got fucked too! Shit did I get fucked! Remember I already told you his dick was bigger than mine, well maybe not twice as big, but believe you me, that night I would have sworn it was! It looked that big, especially when I knew it was gonna be going up in my ass – an ass that had never even been fingered before – and then of course when I felt it, after it was up in there, it felt that big!"

"After I loaded him up with what was probably about a half of a coke can of cum – well shooting out of me it felt like about that much – he told me to lie down on the floor, and he and that telephone pole of his laid down on me and I knew what was gonna happen. I felt him smear some of that lube up in my ass, and that was the very first time that I had ever felt fingers going up in my ass, and then all of a sudden, I felt the tip of his rod knocking right at my ass! He very calmly and softly, told me to just lie there and relax. He knew damn well that I was afraid of what was gonna happen, but yet, he also knew that I was so fucking horny for that rod that I probably would have chewed the nap out of the carpet, trying to keep my mouth shut and not scream or say anything, that sounded like I did not want to do this! He laid his head down right beside my ear, and real softly told me that he had fucked a lot of guys' asses before, and some of them were a whole lot smaller than mine was, and none of 'em ever had any trouble, at all, in taking his dick just as fast as he could feed it to 'em. I tried to tell him, 'Okay,' when all of a sudden, he pushed on my ass and I knew I had just taken the full twelve inches of stiff dark meat! I was getting fucked, and I do mean fucked! That man knew how in the hell to fuck some man's ass to everybody's complete and smiling satisfaction. I sure as hell knew exactly when he hit his point of satisfaction, cause I felt it going up in me in flushes and more flushes, and of course that warm flow of his juices made the whole insides of me, hit my complete and smiling satisfaction! I had just been fucked, hard, in the ass by probably one of the biggest, strongest, most muscled men in Chicago, and I felt like I had just been awarded the top prize, for being able to, 'go for the gusto!'"

"I had been fucked for my first time, and I admitted it immediately that, 'Yes, I loved it, and I knew I'd be getting screwed just as often as possible, but right then, just the lying there under that magnificent body of muscles was almost just as hot as getting fucked, and getting to fuck him. One magnificent hot body! And it still is!"

"And it still is!? Wait! How do you know it still is?"

"Hey! Chicago and St. Louis ain't that far apart! A guy's gotta go to meetings once in a while you know!"

"Oh shit Chase! You mean you and Bro Bubby still do it? You still see each other?"

"Yeah! Sure do! Now remember, Nancy has no idea about that, so please don't say anything. Okay? She knows Bubby, and she knows we are friends, but she sure don't know the rest of it. So just don't let anything slip, okay?"

"Uhhhhhhh, I don't really think I'm gonna be telling Jean about what you and I have been doing, let alone saying anything about what you've been doing! But shit man – maybe I'm a little jealous since it must be that fucking good!"

"Hey, Ben. My talking about getting it in the ass from Bro Bubby is really getting my ole hole hot and anxious. I kinda guess maybe you've never done some guy's ass before, right?"

"No, no I sure haven't. Are you telling me, you want me to fuck you? Is that what you're saying?"

"Yes, hell yes! Interested?"

"Uhhh, yeah I think so. God man – I'm not sure! Hey, I've never done anything with a guy, until with you yesterday, so I don't know. I guess from what you've been telling me about you and Bro Bubby, and the fact that you and he still get together to do it, then I guess maybe I ought to try it. You want me to?"

"Yes, hell yes! I'm not getting any action back home, and it's gonna be about three months before I get a chance to go up and visit the big dick up in Chicago, so yeah, yes, I want you to fuck me!"

"Okay. I guess but if I do something wrong, you gotta tell me, okay?"

"Yeah okay, but it sure is hard to do something wrong. All you gotta do is find my little ole asshole, poke your dick at it, and then punch in! I might jump a little at first when you poke the hole open, but don't worry about that any. That's just getting the ole hole opened up to take your dick, and then it is gonna be a fucking breeze from that point on. Here, I grabbed some hand cream from in the bathroom so we would have something as a lube, so squirt some of that in my asshole, and then maybe some on your dick, and go in! Ready?"

"Yeah, I guess so. About all I can say right now is, from the way I feel after you telling me about you getting fucked by Bro Bubby, I feel like it's only gonna take about two or three pushes in your ass to make me cum like a roaring lion. Chase, I am about as horny right now as I think any man can be! I've never felt this anxious to feel my dick going into something, and yes, I will admit that as a teenage kid, I did try fucking the knot hole in a fence once. So, I guess I'm just trying to tell you that I can have my moments of fantasy too. Ready, I'm gonna go in, I can feel the ring of your asshole on my dick."

"Yeah man, I can feel it too! Push, push! Yeah, yeah – yeah! Oh man, you have just now fucked another guy! How you liking it? Like the way your dick feels up in there? Damn man, it feels good to me! Oh shit, pump me man, pump me! Slam it hard! Don't be afraid of getting kinda rough back there, get rough. You're in a guy's ass right now, not some women's pussy, so fuck it hard! If you've ever wondered what it'd be like to really do some hot and heavy slamming when doing some fucking, now is the time to do it! Bro Bubby pumps me so fucking hard that we have to make sure nobody else is in the house to hear us, so do me man, do me!"

"Oh man, oh! Oh shit man! I'm fucking and pounding on you and this ass of yours as hard as I can! Oh my God man, I have never felt anything like this before! Oh shit man, what a feeling! Oh your ass is so firm and solid, I can just slam the hell out of it! Oh Chase – Chase I'm gonna cum man – I'm gonna cum!"

"Good, good – good! Keep it in me! Keep it in me! Keep pumping on me man, kept pumping! I wanna feel your hot cum hit up inside of me! I wanna feel – ohhhhh, ohhhh man, you just did it, I know! Oh Ben, I can feel you feeding me all your hot cream and milk! Oh man what a great feeling! Oh shit, I am gonna remember this anniversary for one hell of a long time! Oh shit man! God I am so fucking glad you did that! Oh wow! Oh shit! Oh man, that was so fucking good! How you doing? You okay?"

"Oh yeah man, I guess! Oh I am fucking exhausted! Oh my God man – I have never fucked half that hard! Oh Chase, what a fucking ass you've got! Man alive – I don't blame Bro Bubby for doing you as often as he can! What an ass! Shit man, I wish I could be there and watch you get fucked by that big man – and you fucking him too! Oh man, that would be so hot! Oh God I can't imagine seeing both of you hot guys doing each other in bed! Damn man, what a sight that would be! Hot as hell! Oh man, I gotta rest! I gotta get some air! Hey guy, can I just lie here on you for a minute? Oh, I am exhausted!"

"You can lie there just as long as you want! You feel good to me lying there! Try to keep your cock in my ass though as long as you can! It still feels good up in there!"

"Oh it's going soft though! It's exhausted too! Oh man, I had no idea fucking some guy's tight hard ass could feel that good! Thanks Chase, thanks!"

"Hey you are welcome man, you are welcome! Thanks to you for doing me! Once you rest a couple of minutes, you wanna maybe see what it feels like to be the one getting fucked? I'd love to run my dick up in your ass! You interested? You wanna do that?"

"Oh yeah man, yeah, I admit, yeah I do! I think any other day and I'm sure I'd probably scream 'NO!' but after fucking you and also hearing about you and Bro Bubby doing your stuff, I gotta! After I go home, there's no way I will be able to get it done, so yeah, while I've got the chance, I gotta do it. Honestly man, I feel like some kid that is doing everything that his mommy and daddy always told him not to do, and this action, and getting to know you, is really gonna make this trip one special trip, for me. Course, when I'm home and everybody asks how the trip was, it's gonna be damn rough keeping my mouth shut about the most exciting part of it. All I gotta say though, you got one hell of a big rod, and I'm not so sure it's gonna slam up into my asshole like mine did in yours! Chase, if I can't take it, please promise me that you'll stop! Please!"

"Hey man, I promise! I promise cause I know damn well it's gonna go up in your ole ass just as easy as yours went up into mine. But, yes I promise to stop if you think you just cannot do it! Come here. Lie down here where I was and just relax. Remember, I told you about me getting big Bro Bubby's big rod up in my ass for the first time, and I keep going back for more, just as often as I can. Believe me man, there is no way I'd want to be fucking you in the butt if it didn't feel good for you!"

"Okay, okay. I trust you, but like I said, please stop if I can't take it."

And with that statement, I finally shut my mouth and just laid there. I felt big Chase get on top of me, and I felt him fingering my ass, getting me all that much more excited, which yes, I do admit, it worked! In just about two minutes, my ass was jumping up and down, back and forth, just being as anxious as can be imagined, to start feeling something going up in there!

I felt the tip of his dick and I let out an, "Oh shit!" I was just about to get it in the butt, and I knew it! Never before in my entire life had I ever thought that I'd be getting fucked by some guy, and now there I was, on the edge of the big island of Hawaii, lying on the ground of an absolutely beautiful tropical jungle, feeling a man of complete muscle and power lying on my back, and that man getting ready to put his enormous big black dick up in my ass! And I am lying there, mentally yelling for him to, 'Do it! Do it!' I'm a thirty six year old construction worker. I'm a man's man! I'm not some wimp type of a guy! I've been married for sixteen years. I have two teenaged kids. I'm the president of our homeowners association. I'm a regular church attendee and now, for the very first time in my life that I have even thought that something like this could happen, I am mentally begging this big, bold, black, beautiful, muscled hunk of a man to hurry up and put his dick up in my ass! Never, never, had I ever had thoughts of this ever happening, nor of me even wanting it to happen! This was just not what men do together! But oh my God, I needed him, and I needed him up and in there, and I needed it now!

Lying there, nervous and yet anxious as hell, all of a sudden I let out with, "Oh my God you just went in! Oh shit man – oh you've just fucked my ass man, I can tell you just went in! Oh man – push on me man, push! Oh yeah, yeah, oh yeah I can feel it going up in there! I can feel it! Oh damn man – that feels so fucking good! Oh yeah, yeah, push hard, really hard! Fuck me man, fuck me! Yeah do it! Do it!! Do it!!! Oh I am getting fucked and I do mean fucked! Oh Chase – thank you for doing this for me! Oh man, I cannot believe I've actually got your big fucking rod up inside of me! Oh Chase, fuck me man, fuck me!

Oh man, I'm finally getting what I think every man should get some day, and that is the feeling of another big strong man up, inside of himself!"

As Chase was banging the hell out of Ben's ass, all of a sudden he let out with, "Hang tight man, hang tight! Oh shit, hang tight! I'm about ready to load you man, I'm about ready to let your ass have it – oh man – ohhhhhhh. Oh God man, oh shit! Oh man, you just got your first load of good ole hot cum shot up in your ass! Oh Ben, don't ever say you've never had a bomb go off inside of your ass! Oh shit man, oh shit! You have just been fucked and I will tell you, you got fucked hard! Fucking a good fresh virgin ass is always good, and that one was especially good! You've got one hell of a hot ass to be fucking, and I fucked it! Oh man, thank you for letting me do that! Thank you! I gotta lie here a minute and re-coup some. Your ass really took it out of me! Thanks man, thanks!"

"I never, never, never, ever thought I'd even *think* about getting fucked in my ass, let alone actually getting it done to me – but thank you sir! WOW! Never did I ever expect or think that getting some big oversized, sausage dick slammed up in my ass, could feel anything like that! Wow! Thank you man, thank you! Oh seriously, I never thought that I'd ever be fucked in the ass nor even want to be, but one hell of a big thank you man, thank you! What a great feeling! I guess now I really do understand the ole saying, 'The bigger, the better.' I'm sure it can't get any better than that! Chase, I can't really tell you how exciting and fun it's been, doing this stuff with you. I know it's gonna be a onetime thing for me, but I never imagined that I'd ever get a session like this going with anyone, let alone a man that looks and is built like you. You have really put some spark back in my life, and I guess maybe it might be like that first session you had with Bro Bubby. Kind of a life changing experience, right? While we're out here by ourselves, let me emphatically thank you! I gotta say that now, cause once back at the house, we gotta act like all we did was take a walk. Man, what a walk, though!"

———————

Leaving some wonderful vacation place such as "Bob and Sandi's house," and the people that have to be left behind, is never fun! It was time for Chase and Nancy to leave and head for the airport, and the driver was there. All six of us, Bob and Sandi, Chase and Nance, and I and Jean were all in a circle, hugging and saying our goodbyes to Chase and Nancy.

Chase and Nancy gave Bob and Sandi a beautifully framed Hawaiian wall picture as a genuine 'Thank you,' for all of their hospitality and rather new friendship, and all of us again hugged Chase and Nancy just before they got into the car to head across the island to the airport.

"Chase – Jean and I talked about that suggestion you made about me coming up to St. Louis to see a Cardinals game, and I'm definitely gonna do that! I'm gonna check out their schedule, and since I've got me somebody now that can show me around town some, I'm gonna do it! You will kinda take care of me while I'm in town, won't you?"

"You better damn well believe it man – I will! I'm glad I suggested that! I know damn well we can have some fun together, taking in a game and running around like a couple of college boys – out having fun! You just let me know which game you wanna go see, and I'll get some tickets and we'll make it a deal! Hey, if we hit the right date, if he's in town we'll let my buddy Bubby, from Chicago go with us, and we'll make a day of it! The three of us'll all go do the town and have some fun! Looking forward to it man, I am! I know of a great place where we can go have dinner after the game."

And again after the final hugs and handshakes, and a rather strong hug and hand shake between the two men – Chase and me – Chase looked at Nancy, and said, "Well Hon, the car is waiting and I know it's kinda hard to say goodbye to people that you just get to know and kinda get to love, but yeah, we gotta go!"

Then looking over at Bob and Sandi, and Jean and myself, they waved their final good bye! I saw a special look coming directly at me from my man of steel, the man that will be letting another bomb go off in my ass, just as soon as I decide which Cardinals game I want to go see! I will have my own personal escort while in St. Louis, and I definitely will be taking advantage of that escort – and all of his superior services! And you know as well as I do, we will definitely be picking a game when the Chicago Cubs are in town.

As they drove away, I slightly 'thanked' God that it happened to be me and Jean, that Chase and Nancy visited the beach with – and not Tyron and Brian. If those two guys had a chance with that man, there would have been no way for me to find out the true meanings of sexual pleasures – big strong, stiff, sexual pleasures! "Go Cardinals Go! I'm headed your way!"

Big Ole Chad

"What you looking at man!?"

"Chad – what in the hell do you think I'm looking at man!? Your dick! How fucking big is that thing?"

"I don't know man, I don't know!"

"Oh come on man – come on! There's no man alive with a dick that fucking big that hasn't measured it at some time or another! Come on Chad, how big is it?"

"Hey man, why in the fucking hell are you worried about my dick anyway! Jim, you're a married daddy with a wife and two kids, so why in the hell you worried about how big my dick is? You shouldn't even be looking at my dick."

Chad, a black thirty one year old, six foot three, two hundred and forty five pound, former high school football player, and now a truck driver, and his co-worker Jim, a white, forty year old, five foot ten, one eighty five pound warehouse manager were taking a piss beside each other when the question came up, "What are you looking at man!?"

"Come on Chad, let me see it! Turn around here man, turn around!"

"Jim, Jim! What in the hell is going on here man, what in the hell is going on?"

With his own dick out and in his hand, Jim looked up at Chad and said, "Chad, I know. I know about you, and it's about time you know about me. I know you play with guys. I saw you kissing and groping that delivery kid yesterday, out behind that truck. I thought something was gonna happen when I saw you following him out back, and yeah, I admit, I followed and I watched. Chad, I wanted that kid to be me! When you grabbed onto his dick and then gave him that big kiss, I was fucking jealous man, I was!"

"Jim, Jim please! Don't tell anybody you saw that, don't tell anybody! I could lose my job man, I could!"

"Chad! Come on man – I followed you in here when I knew you were gonna have your dick out taking a piss, and I'm standing here telling you I wanna see it, and I'm asking you how fucking big it is, and you think I'm gonna tell anybody about this, or what I saw yesterday!? Either one!? Come on man, we've got ourselves a big secret here, and it's gonna stay that way! Chad, like you just said – yeah, I'm married and I have kids, but you gotta know too, I've played with some guys in the past, and even though it's been a few months since the last time, the very first time I laid eyes on you, I got all horny for some cock again, and it took till yesterday, for me to know that it was really okay for me to tell you what I wanted! Chad, I want that dick! Yes, I admit it man, I do! Somehow, I want us to get together!"

"Oh shit man – you're really throwing me for a loop here man, you are!"

As Jim did continue to stand there and have his own cock in his hand, and he kept looking down and admiring Chad's rod, he asked, "Why? Chad, it's obvious to me that you do guys, you showed me that yesterday, even though you didn't know it, and so today, I'm telling you that I do the same thing and I wanna do it with you!"

Looking around and kinda back over his shoulder, Chad asked, "Has everybody else gone? Did everybody else go home?"

"Yeah Chad, yeah! When Sara left the office, I locked the door so I'd know it was just you and me in here, and then I waited. I figured you'd probably need to come take a piss after you got your paper work done and before you left. And I was right! Thank goodness I was right! Yeah man, it's just you and me, and I really do want us to get to know each other a whole lot better, okay? Come on man, tell me, how big is that thing?"

"Jim, I'm a married guy too! You do know I'm married don't you?"

"No Chad, no! No – I didn't know that! I gotta admit I really don't know much about you, but I've never heard you say anything about having a wife or a family, and then yesterday when I saw you and that guy out in the back, I just assumed that you were a single guy. You do play around with guys, right?"

"Yeah, I do just once in a while. I guess maybe kinda like you, just once in a while. That guy you saw yesterday was a guy that I did happen to meet a few days ago, but he and I have never done anything together. He's like you – he's told me wants to get together, and that's why he was here yesterday. He was trying to get me to come over to his place. The kissing and the grabbing his crotch was cause he asked me to do it, hoping it'd make me want to go with him."

"Oh shit man, I had no idea! Maybe I had you figured out all wrong. But you do, once in a while – right? I mean man, you kissed that guy and you grabbed his dick, didn't you? So I mean, you do play around with guys some, don't you?"

"Well yeah – once in a while!"

"Well, I gotta be honest then, I really do want us to get together! Chad, you turn me on man, you really do!"

"Jim, I don't know where we could go do it. I can't take you home and I kinda figure you can't take me to your place either can you?"

"No, but there is the old warehouse space that we use for extra storage. We've both got keys for it, and we know nobody's gonna be there. The only time anybody is there is when you or I go there to pick up some stuff that's needed here. It's only five minutes from here and hopefully it's on your way home. You do live down by the river don't you?"

"Yeah, yeah I do. But Jim, you really sure that we ought to be doing this? I mean man – we work together and I sure don't want anybody around here finding out that we're doing stuff together."

"I know, I know! I don't want anybody finding out about it either, but hey, as long as you and I both keep our mouths shut, who's gonna find out? Come on man, come on! I wanna play with that thing."

"Well, what're we gonna do if we go there? What kind of playing do you wanna do?"

"Chad my man, I wanna just play with you and that hot body that you've got and especially play with that big long 'slonger' that you've got hanging there on the front of you. I've only played with one other black man before, and I thought he was hot, but man, compared to you, he don't hold a candle. You got one hell of a hot body, and I wanna feel it and play with all of it. Seriously man, from day one when you got hired here, I've driven home after work with a hard-on just thinking about you and what I just knew you had to have hanging in there. That's the reason I followed you yesterday and have been doing that ever since you first got here. I just knew that it had to happen sometime, sometime when I could find out for sure and then be able to tell you how I want some good hot time with you."

"Jim, how long you been playing with guys? You always been doing that?"

"Oh no man, no! I was married for about eight years before anything like that happened. I never knew I was even inclined to play with a man, but when I was a truck driver, and was on an overnight run, things changed."

"Things changed? Like what happened. What changed?"

"I was on Interstate 10 headed for the Los Angeles area, and I was about halfway between Phoenix and the California border. It was in the middle of the summer, and it was hot as hell out there in the desert, and this guy was standing out there alongside of the road – hitch-hiking. No car in sight, nobody else around, and this guy standing out there all by himself, hitch-hiking. Yeah, I admit, I drove past him at first, then all of a sudden I got real concerned about why he was out there with no protection on him from the sun, and so – stupid or smart, I don't know – I hit the brakes and pulled over. By that time I was a little ways down the road, but he saw it and he came a running. I kept watching him in the review mirror and he kept waving like wait, wait, and I, of course, kept wondering if I was being smart or dumb for waiting, or should I be hitting the gas and getting the hell out of there. I waited. He got to the truck, opened the passenger side door, and threw his backpack in on the floor. He was pretty well exhausted from the running and all he could say right then was, 'Thanks man! Thanks!' And then he crawled up into the truck."

"Still pondering my smarts and wondering if I should have picked this guy up or not, I put it in gear, and headed on down the road. I finally looked over at him and asked, 'What you doing out there all by yourself and hitch-hiking out there?'"

"He told me, 'Oh man, what a bad mistake I made. I thought that I'd be okay if I hitch-hiked back home since I'm pretty well broke and don't have a car nor enough money to get a bus ticket, but I sure didn't expect to get a ride with some kook of a guy that I just simply had to get away from. I lied and told him that I needed to head down a road that we were getting close to, and I told him I had to get out. Fortunately he stopped, and yeah, I got out. I decided my chances of survival out along the side of the road were better than being in his car. Nutty as hell! And I mean it! He talked like some real weirdo and drove worse than he talked. So man, I really do appreciate you stopping for me.'"

"I asked him where he was headed for and where he was coming from, and he told me he was coming from Tucson and headed for Oakland. Then he asked me where I was headed for and I told him I was headed for San Fran to drop off a load and pick up another. I guess that kind of broke things for us a little and I decided that maybe I had done the right thing by picking him up."

"Anyway, things went pretty well. Found out he was going to school at a welding school someplace down by Tucson, and was headed home for a couple of weeks. He was twenty-three years old, and yeah, built like a brick shit house. Not like you man, but for a twenty three year old, hot as hell. Of course I did not really notice that until later that night."

"Yeah? Later that night? What happened? He was still with you then?"

"Oh yeah, he was. As we drove and talked, I decided that maybe this kid did need some help and, hell, I was driving that way, anyway. The only thing was, we were gonna have to have a layover just before we got into the LA area. Since I was driving an 18-wheeler with a double bed sleeper in it, I decided no problem. I figured we could share the bed with no problem. So anyway, we stopped at the truck stop, I bought him some supper – like a hamburger, I think – and after watching some TV there in the lounge, we went out to the truck. Everything was fine. We both crawled into bed, and yeah, we kept our briefs on. But hey, I had no reason to even think that having him in bed with me was gonna be any kind of a problem."

"What!? You are telling me about the first time you had sex with a guy – right?"

"Yeah, right."

"Uh, like how old were you at that time?"

"I was twenty eight. So I was a little older than he was. His name was Scott, and I found out later was the big football star when in high school. The man that got all the girls and the girls, in turn, got him whenever they wanted. He was 'The jock!'"

"So anyway, we sacked out about nine thirty and I know I went to sleep right away. I thought he did too, but found out later that if he did or not, he was awake at twelve. And with his hand on my ass!"

"Oh shit! He had his hand on your ass? Did you still have your briefs on?" Chad responded, as he stood there listening to an experience that was getting hotter and hotter as it went. And to Jim's pleasure, since he did notice that as he was talking, Chad's hand had not been removed from grabbing onto his rod, and the rod was not getting any smaller as the conversation when on.

"Yeah, well, I guess maybe kinda. I had 'em on, but he also had his hand kind of stuck down inside of them. I told him, 'Hey Scott, let's not do this. Okay? I don't play with guys like that!' That's when he took his other hand and slid it inside of the briefs too. I sure as hell did not want to start something out there in the parking lot of the truck stop, so I just quietly tried to get him to stop."

"Hey Scott please, please. Let's not! Okay? Let's not. I don't play with guys. I like you and we're having a pretty good time together here on the road, but let's not mess it up by trying stuff that I just do not do. Okay?"

"Hey Jim, nothing bad is gonna happen. I just wanna feel you some and just rub on you. I like feeling your skin. I like feeling your muscles. Just lie there and enjoy my rubbing on you some."

"Okay Scott, I'm gonna just lie here and let you feel me, but that's as far as anything goes – okay?"

"Yeah, yeah. Just let me feel you and kind of rub on you and I think maybe you'll decide that letting me do that is not so bad. Just lie there and let me make you feel good. Okay?"

"Yeah, okay, but understand me man, nothing funny, okay?"

"Yeah Jim, nothing funny, but haven't you ever let a guy play with you some?"

"No Scott, no! No, nobody's ever played with my body, well except for my wife. But then not like some guy would."

"Uhhh, ever kinda wondered what it'd be like to have some guy kinda playing with you?"

"No, no! Well, maybe. Yeah, once in high school I happened to see some guys doing some stuff to each other and then of course I wondered what that would feel like, but that was the only time."

"So tell me. What were they doing?"

"They were goofing around with each other. Not too much cause they were in a locker room and I'm sure they knew somebody could have come walking in on 'em, so not too much."

"Where were you? How did you happen to see 'em?"

"I came around the corner from the massage room, no door to open or close, and I caught 'em feeling each other and kinda playing with each other."

"So how long did you watch em?"

"Oh probably two or three minutes. I just stood there behind some open locker doors and they couldn't see me."

"Two or three minutes!? If you watched for two or three minutes, you had to have seen quite a bit of action. What did they do?"

"Like I said, they kinda goofed around with each other."

"They kinda goofed around with each other? So what kind of goofing around did they do? What did they do to each other? Tell me."

"Well, when I walked around the corner and first saw them, Danny was biting on Chuck's nipple. I gotta admit, I'd never seen somebody chew on a guy's nipple and I guess the way Chuck kept telling him to do it tighter and tighter made me just stand there and watch. First he chewed on one tit, then he moved over and chewed on the other tit. And the whole time Chuck kept telling him to do it tighter and tighter, and harder and harder."

"And you've never had your tits chewed on?"

"No Scott, no!"

"So what else did that Danny and Chuck do while you were watching 'em?"

"Danny was, I guess, maybe the instigator cause he was the one that was doing most of the stuff, although Chuck sure never told him to stop. After he chewed on Chuck's tits some, then he ran his tongue right down his body and licked his body while he rubbed and grabbed his ass cheeks with his hands. He sucked Chuck's dick into his mouth for just a few seconds before Chuck asked him to quit because he was afraid that somebody might come in and see it. So anyway, Danny looked like he sucked on it real hard for about three times, then let it go and stood back up. They both kinda kept looking around some to see if anybody had come in, but they never saw me hiding over in the corner. Then they both grabbed ahold of each other's cocks and stroked 'em back and forth."

"So tell me, how did that make you feel? They both had hard-ons, right?"

"Yeah, of course they had hard-ons. They'd been playing with each other."

"Well, tell me. Did you have a hard-on? You were probably standing there totally nude, or almost nude too, right?"

"Well yeah, I guess I did. I mean, I'd never seen two guys playing with each other like that, so yeah, I got hard."

"And that is the only time that you ever thought about one guy playing with another guy?"

"Well, maybe not the only time. I mean man, once you see something like that, you kinda remember it once in a while after that."

"So tell me about some of the other times that you've remembered it. Like when?"

"Well, to be very honest about it, like right now. I'm lying here in a bed with you, almost totally naked, you've got your hands on me, and rubbing on me, and yeah, being in this situation like this would make me remember it. And I noticed – Scott – that you don't have your briefs on anymore, do you? Why?"

"I'm not used to wearing shorts or briefs when in bed, so I took 'em off earlier. How'd you know that?"

"My hand rubbed up against you when I woke up, and besides, just by looking, I can see you've got a hard-on and it's pushing up on the sheet. Right?"

"Yeah, right. But let's get back to you, and how often do you think about letting some guy give you a good body rub. You ever get a massage?"

"Yeah. Yeah I do once in a while."

"By a male masseur or a woman masseur?"

"Both. Either male or female, not always the same person.

"Which do you like the best?"

"I don't know. Either one I guess?"

"Ever kind of feel excited when a male masseur does you? Ever feel like maybe he could reach down, like maybe between your ass cheeks and give you a rubbing down in there a little deeper? Like maybe really give your butt cheeks a good tight squeezing?"

"Yeah, yeah. I've thought that a few times. Thought that probably would feel good."

"Ever felt that way when a lady is giving you the massage?"

"Well probably. Yeah, I assume, probably."

"But you're not so sure are you? You are sure about it if it is a man, but not so sure about a woman, are you?"

"I guess not. Yeah, I guess maybe you are right. Gotta admit I've never wanted some gal to slide her hands down in there, but have thought it might feel really good if a guy did it. Yeah, you're right."

"Okay then man, tonight you are gonna see what that feels like. Okay?"

"Oh Scott, I don't know! You're trying to tell me that you want to massage down in my ass, right? You're wanting to squeezed my butt cheeks, aren't you?"

"Yeah, hell yeah! You've already told me that you've wondered just what that would feel like, and right now you are with a guy, here in bed with you that wants to do it and let you see how it feels. Don't say anything. Just lift up your butt and let me slide these briefs off of your ass and then just lie there and relax."

"But Scott – Scott. Hey man, I'm not so sure about this. Yeah, I know I told you that I had thought about some guy doing that to me once in a while, but seriously man, I'm not sure we should be doing this. You gotta remember I'm a little older than you and I've got a wife and kids at home, and really man, I'm not so sure we should. I just don't play with guys."

"I hear ya man, but listen. You've already admitted that in the past you've wanted someone to do this for you, but it's never happened, and right now it can happen. It's just you and me in here, and listen, you may never get another chance to see what a good ass rubbing can feel like. Seriously man, this is a great chance to finally see what it can feel like. Nobody but you and I are gonna know a damn thing about it or that it even happened. Hey, just lie there and let me do the rubbing and give me a chance to let you see how great it feels to have a good strong hand rub your butt cheeks a little."

"Oh God man! Okay Scott, but just rubbing my butt some, okay? Nothing funny man, just rub my ass some and then that's it, okay?"

"Yeah man, yeah. Let me pull your underwear off and you just lie there. Once we start, I think you're gonna be pretty glad we're doing this. Just relax man – just relax."

"I'm trying to, I'm trying to – but Scott you gotta understand that I've never had some guy putting his hand up in there like you're doing right now. Hey, you are putting your hand up in there, aren't you? I can feel your fingers sliding up in between my butt cheeks. I can feel that Scott, I can feel that. Oh Scott, yeah man, I gotta agree, that does feel pretty good. Yeah, it does feel a little different than anything I've ever felt before. Oh yeah, I can feel you moving your fingers around back there.

Yeah, maybe – maybe just a little deeper. Yeah, oh yeah! Oh shit Scott, you are right! Oh man, I never felt anything like this before. Yeah man, yeah! Yeah, put your hand down in there. Yeah – yeah – go just a little bit deeper, yeah oh yeah, just a little bit more man. Oh yeah – that does feel good! Oh God Scott, squeeze it man, yeah go ahead – yeah, yeah – squeeze it. Oh shit man – thank God you talked me into this! Yeah Scott – I gotta agree now. This does feel great. Yeah, no masseur ever made my ass feel this good!"

"Hey Jim, just lie still there. I'm gonna lie down on top of you so you can feel me on you – from top to bottom. I wanna just lie down on you. Yeah man, oh yeah! Oh yeah this feels good! You okay? You okay man?"

"Yeah Scott, yeah I am. I gotta admit man, you sure as hell were right! You're making me feel damn good. Oh Scott, I've never had a man lying down on top of me like this. Wow, this does feel good. Yeah, yeah! Yeah, do that! Yeah, move around on me some. Let me feel you all over me man, let me feel you! Oh shit man, that feels so fucking good! You feel so good on top of me. Oh Scott, I never imagined that having a guy lying on top of you – all skin to skin – could feel anything like this."

"Feels good don't it? I told you it would feel good. Glad you're finally letting me feel you, aren't you? Feels good don't it?"

"Oh yeah, yeah! Oh yeah, and I think right now, I can feel something else going on back there, don't I? What're you doing Scott? What are you doing?"

"Yeah, yeah just a little more action. Just lie still there man, we're gonna let you find out now, how hot and good it feels to have a little dick slide up and in you! Just lie there and let me take care of you. I know damn well you've always wondered what it'd feel like to feel some guy's dick going up and in you, and I'm gonna let you find out, okay? You've always wondered haven't you? Specially after watching those two guys in the locker room playing with each other, right? You just knew that those two guys fucked each other didn't you? You didn't see it, but you knew they did that to each other, didn't you?"

"Hell yeah man, hell yes. I just as well gotta admit to you that yes – I've wondered about that for a long time, and Scott, I guess maybe you are the one that is going to show me what it feels like, cause you've got me so fucking hot putting your hand up in my ass like that, and now, I know damn well that you've got your dick right there at my asshole, don't you? You're ready to poke it in me aren't you? I'm gonna get fucked, ain't I? Ain't I!?"

"Yeah man – yeah! Hey, you're helping me out by giving me a ride, and so I'm gonna help you out by letting you finally find out just how fucking good it feels, to let some guy slide his dick up in your ass. Tonight's your chance to do something that you've wondered about for years, and if you don't do it tonight, it could be a lot of years before you get another chance. Yeah man, lie still there and let me fuck you. You are gonna kiss me for this when we get done."

"And Chad, I did. I just laid there and finally let the guy do what he wanted to do and I gotta admit, I enjoyed it. He massaged my butt and then he fucked my butt, and I guess that got me all turned on, because before the night was over, I got fucked and I got sucked off, too. I had to admit after that night was over that I had been looking forward to a night like that for years. I had just been constantly rejecting it as a possibility, but when it happened, then I knew I had been wanting it, and now that I stop and think about it, since I've never told anybody else about that day – and that night – maybe that is the hidden reason that I stopped and picked him up along the highway. Maybe, internally, I knew he was a hot looking guy, and maybe I was secretly hoping that something like that could happen, and it did! Oh boy, did it!"

"So he fucked you and he sucked you off that night, right?"

"Yeah, yeah he did. He fucked me and gave me my very first blowjob. Gotta admit that if I had not been looking for something like that to happen, I'm sure I would never have let him do it, but once he played with my ass and then turned me over and sucked me off, then it was all go! I didn't suck him off that night, but I sure did the next night. After that night, I made arrangements for us to spend the next night together in San Fran."

"So tell me Jim. When he fucked you that night, you did enjoy it, I guess? You liked it?"

"Oh hell yes! Yeah, for getting a cock up in my ass for the very first time, I sure did beg for it deeper and rougher, and again, deeper and rougher! I found out that night that I'm a true bottom – as they say – for a big rod, and Chad, that is just what in the hell got me so excited when I finally got to see yours."

"So I guess maybe you're telling me that when we get together, you want me to push this thing up in your ass, right?"

"Oh hell yes! Shit yes man, hell yes! Just you standing there and kinda stroking it back and forth, just like you've been doing the whole time we've been standing here, is making my ass twitch like crazy. It's been months since I've had any dick up in there, and it's been one hell of a long time since I've had one that even comes close to the size that you've got, so hell yes, I want that thing up in me just as far as it can go. I want the whole damn thing up in me. I wanna feel it all the way up in there!"

"Jim, I gotta tell you that I've had guys beg off of it since it ended up being a little more than they could take. You sure you can take the whole thing? Cause, I gotta tell you man – if you can – then maybe I have finally found me a man that I can use once in a while, when I need to really slam something. I have to be really slow and soft when I and Judy get together. She told me once that if we had had sex before we got married, the size of my rod might have made her change her mind. I've had way too many guys that said they wanted it, but then as soon as the head of it slips in, they start screaming that they can't take it, they make me pull back out, and then leave me high and dry without getting any good ass. I've been looking for an ass that can take it all the way and a guy that wants more and more of it. Maybe you and I can make each other happy."

"Chad, you never had sex with Judy before you got married?"

"No. I had learned my lesson about guys and gals wanting to back out once they either saw it or once they tried to take it. I've never even found me a man that can take the whole thing down in his throat and give me a complete blow job."

"So Chad, when did you first have sex with a man? What happened? I know you've had sex with women before, but I gotta be honest and tell you, I wanna hear about you and some of the guys that you've fucked. Tell me. Tell me about some of your fucking other guys!"

"Okay, you wanna hear about my very first time with a guy?"

"Yeah, yeah! Yeah, tell me what happened and all that stuff. Okay?"

"Well, I was just about twenty years old. Just about a month before my twentieth birthday. I worked at a lumber company then, loading and unloading lumber and other stuff. Well anyway,

I took the city bus to and from work. I noticed once, that there was this one guy that kinda always ended up on the same bus as I did, and he'd always nod and quietly say, 'Hi,' as he got on the bus. Then sometime later, I realized that the same guy was also getting on the same bus that I was on, later in the day, when I was going home from work. Well anyway, one day on the way home, he got up from his seat where he had been sitting and he sat down beside me. We talked a little about nothing in specific, and then for the next few days or a week or so, he always made sure he sat beside me. I did notice that he often looked down, as if to look at my crotch. But I didn't think too much about it. I've always kind of had some trouble keeping it tucked back in, so that it didn't show too much, even if I did have long pants and maybe a coat on. I've never been able to wear boxer shorts. It hangs down my leg and always shows. I always have to wear briefs so I can tuck it up and under some. So anyway, then one evening he was already on the bus when I got on and he motioned for me to come sit beside him. It was kinda back toward the back of the bus and there weren't very many people back there. After we were there for a few minutes I noticed he looked around as if to see who was close by, and I guess noticing that section was pretty well empty, he definitely looked down at my crotch and he put his hand on my crotch, and made sure it was on my dick and then said, 'I've heard about this thing.' I, of course, looked at him with one hell of a big quizzed look on my face. He didn't move his hand. He left it there and then said, 'I'm gonna get off with you.' Then he softly patted my crotch, and kind of slightly squeezed my dick. I didn't say anything but did sit there wondering just what in the hell was happening. We got to my stop, and yes, he got off with me. We only walked a few feet before he told me:"

"I'm Susan's brother. I know you. You're Chad. You and she had a date about a month ago. The next day she told her friend Maryanne about your dick. They were in the living room and I was in my bedroom, but I could hear 'em talking through the register. They didn't know I could hear 'em, but I often sit close to the register and listened to whatever is being said in the living room. Especially if it's Susan and somebody. She told Maryanne how big your dick is. She told her it is really, really big! She told her that you almost could not use it on her because of how big it is. I wanna see it and I wanna play with it. I like to play with guys' dicks. And the bigger, the better!"

"Uhhh, what is your name?"

"Rickie. I'm Susan's brother. The girl you almost couldn't screw cause of the size of your dick. I wanna see it and play with it. I figured that if Susan said it is big, then it's gotta be big! I managed to kinda find out who she had a date with, and I made sure you were the right guy, and I've been planning this for weeks now. I found out what bus you used going to work and which bus you used coming home from work, and I knew where and at what times you got on and off of the bus."

"Hey wait here a minute! I don't play with guys. Why do you think I'd let you play with it, or even see it?"

"Cause I know that guys that have big dicks like for other guys to see it and play with it. I know when a guy wants it played with. Susan told Maryanne that you told her about how the guys in the shower room and locker room used to look at it and try to grab it and you wouldn't let 'em do it, but you admitted that if one of them had grabbed onto it, you think you would have probably let him play with it, just to see what it felt like. And you told her that you thought it might have been fun to let some guy play with it, especially while the other guys watched. You told her that it never happened, but you kinda wished it had. You thought it might be fun to have the other guys watching since you knew you had the biggest dick of any of the guys, and yeah, you wanted 'em to see it all hard and stiff. You also told her that someone put a picture of it on a web site, but even though someone told you where to sign on to see it, you never found out who posted it, nor when they took the picture. You know it's yours though, because of the star tattoo that you have right there beside it."

"But Rickie, those are the old days. That was years ago. Things change."

"Yeah, I know things change, but I know your dick is still the same, and I know that if you wanted guys to watch it get played with back then, you'd still like for some guys to watch somebody doing stuff with it today. Right? You'd still like to have it played with by a guy, wouldn't you. And you'd still like to have other guys standing around watching it get played with. You want 'em to see it all hard and stiff and really sticking out, don't you? Hey, Chad, look down. You're showing a tent standing out down there, right now. Our talking is getting you all excited, ain't it?"

"Well maybe, kinda. I've never stood on a street corner with some guy that I did not even know and talked about my dick and what happened in the shower room. Yeah, I admit that the idea of having somebody watch me and somebody else having sex together, is kind of exciting sounding, but you're a guy, not a girl. I don't play with guys."

"But you'd like to, right? You're too hot of a looking man with an enormous outstanding cock to even try and hide the fact that you'd like to be the center of attention, with a girl, or a guy. I want to help you show it off. I want to be the guy that plays with you while other guys stand around and watch and wish they were doing what I am doing right then. I know damn well that you'd love to be getting played with and knowing that a whole bunch of guys are there, looking at you and your cock and watching it get played with by some guy, and knowing that each one of them wants a chance at you! You'd love to have your body and your cock be the center of attention, and knowing people are there watching you get it taken care of."

"Okay, okay! Your idea sounds kind of exciting – I admit – but just where in the hell could this ever happen? And if you had a place to use, and could set this up, just who are the 'other guys' gonna be? Where you gonna find them?"

"Hey, who the other guys are is no problem at all! I know a whole bunch of guys that would love to be there watching you do it with a guy, and especially if it's your first time. They're all dick lovers that would even pay you good money for just the chance to grab onto that thing and maybe kiss it too. You're standing there with a woodie and un-concisely rubbing it, to the point where anybody coming by could see you doing it, so I know damn well you are game, and now it's just getting it set up so you can finally do something that you've wanted to do for years. That's the reason you even tell your dates about what happened back in school. Doing that is exciting to you ain't it?"

"Okay, okay! Yes, I will admit that doing something like that is a turn on. So if something like this could happen, just how you gonna set this up? When, where and what's gonna happen, if you can set this up?"

"There's a small gym downtown that one of 'our guys,' as in gay guys, owns and he's already told me that if I can get you to agree to this, we can use his place after it closes for the night, and that way, whoever wants to, or needs to, can take a shower after the activity."

"This guy – he knows me?"

"No, no! He just knows about you and he's anxious to see that rod of yours, too. I know of at least twelve guys that are praying that I can get this set up, so you are definitely gonna be showing it off to a number of guys. Guys like me that love big dark cocks, and so everyone of them is gonna be wishing he was the guy, that's playing with you. You've admitted that you wished you could have done some public sex with some guy in the past, well now is the time. I'm gonna have a car come pick you up, so that we know you have transportation downtown and back, and everything will be there and ready. You do not need to bring anything. This coming Friday night. About nine PM, okay? Don't plan on backing out, cause if you do, your name is gonna be all over town, and with the pictures on the web – that we know how to get to – that star tattoo is our guarantee that you will be there."

"Any questions?"

As Chad continued to stand there and did continue to hide his actions of rubbing his crotch, he asked, "Yes one. Can you and I go someplace right now and let me have at least one practice run, of playing with a guy, so that I don't come across as too inexperienced Friday night? And besides, I'm sure you're gonna want my dick up in your ass Friday night while all of your buddies are watching, so I think we oughta do a practice run so you know what to expect, okay? I know you've felt it before, cause you did that on the bus, but I'm not sure you've ever had a rod the size of mine up in your cute little ass just yet, so I think we'd better make sure it fits. When I'm in the process of fucking you in front of those guys Friday night, I want each and every one of them wishing it was their asses that was getting my pole pushed up inside. I don't want any of them being glad that it's not their asses that are getting abused. If I'm gonna be around guys that like to get it up in the ass once in a while, I wanna be damn sure I'm the guy they all want doing it, to 'em. Come on, let's go find someplace where we can do our 'practice run,' cause

I gotta find out what having sex with a guy, instead of a girl, is like. Hope like hell your ass is big and open. You better not yell at me like the girls do and tell me that it's too big, and you can't take it. You asked for it, and you're gonna get it! Never done a guy before, but hey, maybe you're my solution to all of the, 'No! I can't take it,' yellings."

    "Oh shit Chad, did that guy get it set up for you, to do that? Did he take it okay? Did you fuck his ass that day?"

    "Oh yeah, he took it and he got the Friday night thing all set. Thank goodness, though, that we did do the 'practice run,' thing. He admitted that he's taken some pretty damn big dicks ever since he started playing around with guys about four or five years earlier, but he told me that taking mine for the first time, it was a 'challenge.' He told me later that he really had to keep his mouth shut to keep from screaming when it went up in him. But it was a challenge that paid off well. I used him for a lot of times when I was needing some sex and I was just not getting any from the gals. There were a lot of nights when something did not work out so well for me with some date, and hey, I'd give him a call and tell him that I needed some attention and show up at his place and then leave the next morning. There was not one night, when he ever turned me down. We even had some damn good three ways, when he already had someone at his place when I called, needing help. Honestly man, I just about gave up on having sex with dates. I used Rickie and his buddies for getting my rocks off. That's why I didn't initiate having sex with Judy until our wedding night. I kept telling her it was because I had so much respect for her, but actually it was because I was getting it from

Rickie and his buddies, and I really didn't want Judy to see it until after we said the "I dos."

"Hey Chad, the Friday night thing. What happened? Tell me what went on that night."

"Sex! Yeah, sex. Everybody there knew they were there to see some guy's dick that was supposed to be bigger than any they had ever seen, and I guess maybe it worked out that way. There were fourteen guys there besides Rickie and me. It all started off kind of calmly. We all got undressed, and yes, I had an immediate boner sticking out. The whole idea that everything was happening there because, these guys wanted to see my dick, of course, that made me horny as hell. I'd been naked in a shower room or a locker room with guys before, but never in a room where the whole purpose was to be there to watch me and my dick. I almost felt like a circus act, but I'm gonna be honest with you and tell you that I was really turned on. I had to admit that yes, for years, I had been wanting to be the center of attention with people standing around, looking at my body and my dick. And especially when it's good and hard and sticking out, all the way, in front. And then of course, them being there and watching me having sex with someone was a real high to me. Right then I really did not care if it was a guy or a girl that I was fucking around with. It was all just letting people watch me having sex. After that night, I guess I've had to admit that maybe – just maybe – I am an exhibitionist."

"Well holly crap Chad! If ever there was a more perfect person to be an exhibitionist, I don't know who in the hell it could be! You've got the body of glory on you – every part of you is like a bronze statue – and then of course that dick is enough to make any person sit up and take notice. It's so big, bold, black, and beautiful, just like the rest of you. So that Friday night, that Rickie guy got fucked by you too, I assume?"

"Oh hell yes! Yes, he got fucked, and then just about half of the rest got fucked by me, and the rest all went off running like I was gonna push a dynamite stick up in their asses. They fucked each other, but they were just like the dates I'd had. 'Oh NO! No, no! I can't take that thing!' It sure didn't take me long that night to find out just which guys I could and would be meeting up with again. One guy – forget his name – he begged and begged me all night to fuck him again. I think I fucked that same guy four times that night. For a guy – meaning me – that, until just a few days before, had never played with a guy and his ass, I sure did make up for lost time that night! I started out with Rickie, which was the plan, and then it was 'line 'em up' and let me at 'em. It was like running cattle through the corral gate. Do one, and the next one was there and waiting. I did have one guy that really did have some trouble, but he was insistent that he was gonna take it all the way, and he hung in there until he finally took the whole thing. I was kinda glad that gym place was not real close to other open places that night, cause that guy was not quiet when he was fighting to get my dick up in him. I remember one guy stuffed a rag in his mouth once and told him to try and quiet down. I fucked him again then later, like about a year later, and I guess he had gained some experience, cause that time, he took it like a pro. No screaming and hollering, just one big empty hole that was begging for it faster, harder, and deeper the whole time I was up in him."

"So, other than the, 'you fucking about everybody,' anything else happen that night?"

"Oh yeah. Yeah, plenty of stuff, but probably the most meaningful, was me getting fucked too."

"Whoa! You got fucked that night too!?"

"Oh yeah, yeah. Some of the guys got to saying stuff like, 'He likes to fuck, but can he take it?' And then someone bet another guy that since I was a top, he bet that I wouldn't let anybody in my ass, and of course that meant the challenge was on! I looked at Rickie and asked him, 'Okay, now what do I do?'"

"He looked back as me and asked if I wanted to get fucked or not, and I, of course, said, 'Yeah, I do.' Then he told me to pick out the guy I wanted to fuck me, get some grease up in my ass, and to grease up the guy that I had picked. I figured this whole night was happening almost because I wanted people to watch me having sex, so getting my ass rammed should be part of it. I'd been fucking guys all night, so why not let them see me getting it in the ass, too?"

"How'd you decide who got to fuck you?"

"Well, kinda by just a simple pick and choose. There was this one guy by the name of Ernie, tall, damn good looking black man, just about my age, was built like a brick shit house, and he had let me fuck his ass like some Royal King! I loved the way he let me pound on his ass and so I decided that maybe he'd take care of me the same way. I asked him if he wanted to fuck me, and be the first guy to ever fuck me, and thank goodness he said, 'Yes!' Well, when I was fucking him earlier, I didn't see his dick all out and hard – he was lying on it – but man, I found out from him what a really big dick, up in your ass, feels like. The more he fucked me, the harder and the stiffer it got! And of course, that was the very first time I'd ever been fucked in the ass, and so his load of cum felt like a gallon of juice hitting my insides. I had never thought about what it might feel like to get loaded with some cum juices, but I sure as the hell found out real quickly that night. And he must have been real ready, cause he shot off fast. He loaded me, then laid down on top of me and told me to just lie there, cause he was not done yet. And believe me, he wasn't! Once he caught his breath, he pounded on me, and pounded on me like he was trying to build up enough cum to 'finally' shoot off for the first time! I'm not sure how many times that guy could cum in one night, but I know I got it from him a total of three times, before that night was over. The first time – the real quick time when we first started – then after he caught his breath and pounded my ass for about ten or fifteen minutes, and then we went back at it again, just before we all left."

"Oh man. Except for you playing with that Rickie a few nights before, this was your first time of playing with a guy's ass, and then having someone playing with your ass, right?"

"Yeah, you're right. And I gotta admit, that playing with Rickie earlier in the week was not too much playing. We went to his place, went in down the alley and into the back, and we went into a tool shed. No lights on, but then there was still a little bit of daylight still showing outside. He dropped his Levi's, put some conveniently hidden grease up in his ass, leaned over the work bench, and told me to poke him. In, out, and all done in probably three minutes. At least we knew he could take my dick with no problems, but then I think he already knew that. He did act like my dick was, maybe though, the biggest thing he'd ever put up in there. I found out later, like months later, that he had then gotten into getting fisted. So I kinda guess taking something big back there was definitely all for him. But that night when we talked out on the street corner, he didn't tell me that maybe he was wanting to start getting fisted. I kinda think that might have been one of his main objectives of getting fucked by me – to see if he could take something big up in his ass. Hell man, he could have just bought a big dildo and used it, but then – right – I would have been a much cheaper experiment. Maybe he did then, and used it after I fucked him, just so that he was more used to getting something big put up in there before that Friday night. I know that he sure didn't want to have any problems taking my rod that Friday night. He wanted to be able to take it deep and fast since he was gonna be getting fucked in front of all of his friends. Or maybe he used the blunt end of a baseball bat to do some practicing with, cause on that Friday night, he sure did take me fast and easy.

"Oh shit Chad, I guess maybe you've had a lot more gay sex than I've ever had. Before you got married, I guess you must have used your guy friends quite a bit, right?"

"Yeah, I've pretty well 'done the round,' so to say. Fucking a guy's ass or getting fucked by some good strong big dick is always more fun to me than the standard heterosexual thing. But if you're gonna have kids, then you gotta have the ole wifey thing. I grew up in a very strong religious church family, and living the good ole traditional heterosexual life style is just plain required. Fortunately, being a truck driver, and having the necessity of being out of town once in a while is a blessing. I've got my favorite trips that I volunteer for as often as possible, cause I've got me some 'secret stash,' so to say, in each of those towns. And I don't mean drugs when I say 'stash,' but what I've got there and waiting for me to show up, is a hell of a lot better than drug stash. Doing the driving to just get there can be pretty boring, but man, once I get there, everything changes, and by the time I head back home, I've had me some good time, and I've got my ole body all calmed back down so I can just drive in some nice peace and quiet, and look forward to my next road trip!"

"Hey Chad, make sure that door is locked."

"Yeah, I did. Hey, what you got there? Where'd that come from?"

"Hey man, I've got me a little secret storage space back there behind that old stuff, and so we're gonna have all the comforts of home. A nice fluffy comforter that we can lie on, some good ole ass creaming jell, some paper towels and some towels so we can kinda wipe ourselves clean before we head home to the wives."

"Shit man! I gotta guess then, that this is not the first time you've used this old warehouse for some playing around is it?"

As Jim spread out the comforter and placed the jell and the other items on the floor beside it, he started striping his clothes off and replied,

"No not the first time, and now that you and I have a much better understanding of each other, I'm hoping like hell it gets used a whole lot more."

Chad followed Jim's lead and stripped everything off. And as he did, Jim just stood there in amazement and shock as he finally, for his first time, got to see all of Chad's big black stiff rod sticking straight out and not partly covered with some pants.

Chad finished dropping his clothes to the floor, looked up at Jim, moved his left foot to the left slightly, placed his hands on his waist, and said, "Okay Jim, you said you wanted to see it – there it is. This is me. This is me all naked, bare and showing everything I've got to show."

"Oh my God Chad, you are beautiful, absolutely fucking beautiful! Your whole body is a God. I knew you had a great body and build on you, but man, to see it all standing there completely bare and raw, it is more than a man can imagine! Chad, you are beautiful man, absolutely beautiful!"

"Thanks man, but you sure ain't nothing to sneeze at either. Now that I get to see you, all in the bare and raw, all I can say is, you need to get yourself some new uniforms. You've got a hot body Jim, but with the uniform pants that you wear, nothing shows. And you got a good dick too! That's a good dick! Honestly man, you need to tighten up some of your clothes. Ever since we've met I thought you were nice guy, but there was no way in hell that I could see, that once you got undressed, that you were gonna be showing a body like that, and yes – a dick like that. It may not be a black man's dick, but honestly Jim, I've played with some black dicks that are a lot smaller than yours."

Having made his profound statement about how good Jim looked all bare and naked, Chad dropped to his knees, grabbed Jim by the legs, pulled him forward and swallowed his rod.

Jim responded with, "Oh man, oh man. Oh Chad thanks man, thanks! Oh that feels so good. Oh it's been way too long since I've had a man down there sucking on that thing, and this is feeling great! Oh Chad suck it hard man, suck it hard! Thanks man. Thanks!"

As Jim stood there and Chad took care of the white nine inch hot dog that Jim was supporting, all of a sudden he started uttering with some 'oh's' and some 'ah's', and then they got louder and more rapid, and as Jim grabbed ahold of Chad's head and pulled him in closer, he was emphatically almost yelling, "Oh it's coming Chad, it's coming! I'm gonna cum man, I'm about to cum! I'm cumming man – I'm cummmmmin! Oh shit man, oh shit! Oh Chad, I have not had a climax like that in years. Thanks man, thank!"

As Jim was attempting to come back down from his climax heaven, Chad slid back slightly, and off of Jim's cum coated cock. He leaned forward toward Jim's body and silently licked all of Jim's conveniently available skin. For more than three or four minutes, Chad continued to kneel there, in front of Jim, and almost worship all and any parts of Jim's torso. Jim simply stood there, touching so softly Chad's shoulders and raising his head up toward the sky as if to be thanking some 'one' or some 'thing,' for the feelings that he was experiencing.

Slowly Chad sat back, took a deep breath, looked up at Jim, smiled and said, "Thanks man, thanks!"

Looking down at Chad, grinning, Jim asked, "Thanks!? Why are you thanking me man? You are the one that just gave me the blowjob of the century. I need to be thanking you! Why are you thanking me?"

Still kneeling back on his heels, Chad looked up at Jim and replied, "Cause man, I think you and I just hit some kind of a new companionship that I have never had with any of my players, and yeah, even my wife. Jim, I honestly cannot explain it, but I'm feeling good feelings that I have not had for years, and really maybe never have had. I've never had sex like that before. Every time I'm with a guy, he's just all over me and he really does not care if I'm enjoying what is happening or not! Yeah, him being all over me and feeling me, it feels good, but I never feel like we are really connecting. I just feel like a big rag doll to be rolled around and played with. You know, now that I think about it, I think it goes all the way back to that Ricky guy and all of his friends using me and just having their fun. Yeah, yeah I admit I liked being the center of attention and having a bunch of guys watching me have sex, but I really do think that was just kind of a reaction to, and a rejection for all of the church stuff that I had to live through, when I was a kid. Honestly man, I'm still living that stuff today. I'm trying to live a heterosexual life style just because that's what's required, but Jim I shouldn't be married. Yeah, I told you that Judy and I never had sex before we were married, and I used the excuse that I didn't want her to see the size of my dick until after we were married, and yes, I told myself that was the reason, but no – that's not the reason – I'm just not supposed to be married. I'm living a lie, man, I know I am!"

Jim sat down on the comforter facing Chad and put his hand on Chad's upper leg. Chad sat down on the floor, beside and facing Jim.

Silently Jim sat there for a few minutes, looking at Chad and his mournful face and finally said, "I'm with you Chad, I'm with you! I know what you're saying and I know how you're feeling. You're not alone man, you're not alone. All too many of us are living lives that are not really real. I didn't discover my true self until after I was married, and that was because where I came from, that was just the required thing to do. I came from a real small farming town, and hey, if you were getting a little older, and still unmarried, then the town talked. And they didn't talk nice."

"Chad, how long you and Judy been married?"

"Six years. Six years."

"Any kids Chad?"

Looking over at Jim and shaking his head 'no,' Chad did respond. "No! Thank goodness no kids. You know Jim, to have kids you gotta be doing the old straight sex thing, and we just don't do that too much. Never really have. I did it when I was younger and of course while in high school as the big football star, but I guess once that thing with Ricky and his friends happened, I started looking the other way – well that is until every so often the whole family would almost all get together to ask me just when was I gonna get married, and who was I gonna marry. The same ole family pressure!"

Silently sitting there, both men still fully nude, Jim slightly squeezed Chad's leg just enough to silently let him know that, "I'm still here with you man, I'm here."

"How is your relationship with Judy? You two getting along okay?"

Just slightly raising he head up some to just almost look at Jim's eyes, Chad softly said, "Oh, yeah kinda of I guess." Then shaking his head slightly, he continued, "Hell, I don't know. I honestly don't feel for her like I just felt being down there in front of you and hearing you get all excited about what I was doing for you. Seriously Jim, I just don't have any feelings at all when she and I do have sex, and to me, it's more like, 'Hey let's just get this over with.' And when I have sex with guys, like I said, It's almost always about them, and making sure they're getting what they want. You know, you can only pound some guy in the ass so many times before it's time to move on. They never ask me if I wanna get pounded. They never ask me if I wanna suck on their dick. They want my dick up in their ass, and they want my dick down in their throat, and as soon as they've had that, it's all happy and, 'I've gotta get going.' Yeah, I know I've got a big dick, but you know, once in a while I wish it was just normal sized so that people – well guys anyway – could find more of me, than just a dick."

"Hey Chad, before today, how long's it been since you sucked some guy off? When did you do that last?"

"Three months ago. I was on a road trip up toward Chicago, and I stopped in a restroom to take an honest piss, and when I was finishing up washing my hands, this cute little wrestler type of a guy came walking in, I looked at him, he looked at me, he grabbed his crotch and acted like he wanted to hand it to me, so I moved him into one of the toilet booths, took his pants down, took his dick out, put my mouth on it and sucked it dry. Three minutes max, and I was out of there, and he was taking a piss. I have no idea who he was, he has no idea who I am, but I got what I wanted, and if he wanted what I have, we will never know, cause he never even felt it."

"You know Chad, I'm feeling kinda of shitty right now, cause I guess I have been acting like all of your other playmates, and that was trying to get to your dick. I'm sorry man, I am."

Popping his head up and looking directly at Jim, Chad quickly responded, "Hey no man, no! Well yeah, I guess maybe you were after my rod, but Jim, for some other reason, you and I are just different together than just some guy wanting to get it up in the ass or down the throat. I'm the one that should have been tracking you and trying to get in your pants, but man, the pants you wear are a total camouflage! You gotta change to some pants that grab your ass and maybe show some of that stick you got up front there. Shit man, when you stripped, my ole log went hard immediately. I knew I was gonna be getting me some of that, and finally I felt like I was getting what I wanted, instead of what someone else wants. And I got it! How damn long has it been since you let some good ole cum fly? It hit me like a cannon ball when you fired off! Damn man, I liked that!"

"Well hey guy, it's been awhile. You know, middle age, family man and that whole thing, sex just ain't as often as it used to be. I'm glad you liked it. Now, on to the other problem, your ass! Still want me to slide my little poker up in there? Today we do things that you want. You got a dick and some cum down your throat, and so now let's put a dick up in that ass of yours. I'll get my turn later on, during our next get together. Cause man, if I can do something for you today that you do not usually get, I'm all for it. I know this is not going to be our only time. Lie down there big man, I'm gonna play with that ass like you ain't never had before! It's gonna get poked and it's gonna get eaten! It's gonna be like when I go in a restaurant and order chicken and they ask if I want white meat or dark – today it is definitely gonna be some dark meat – and I am damn sure it is gonna be some delicious, dark meat."

———————

"Chad, how's it going at home lately?"

"Well Jim, not so good, I guess. You know, since you and I have been meeting here and doing the good stuff, I guess maybe Judy has figured out that I'm getting my rocks off someplace beside our bedroom. She's acting kind of like, 'Well man, just what is going on? We sure aren't headed for the bedroom very often nor very fast, so what's up?'"

"Chad, has she actually asked you if you're getting it someplace else?"

"No, not straight right out. I'm kinda thinking that she's wondering about what I'm doing on my out of town trips."

"She don't expect anything going on around here though?"

"No, I really don't think so. We've been pretty good at picking the right times for us to meet here and do our thing. I don't think she's suspicious of anything while I'm in town, but after I get home from a road trip, then she kinda asks me a lot about what did I do while I was gone."

"Well, that is a good question. What has been happening? Anything good and juicy, as they say?"

As Chad stripped down to his hot bare skin, laid down on the blanket and let Jim mount him and spread his ass cheeks open so that Jim could slide his face up in 'there' and start nibbling, Chad said, "Oh yeah! On my way up to Detroit, I had to take a piss and it paid off real good! I don't usually have to make some pit stops along the road, but that day I did. So I found myself a roadside rest area, about forty or forty five miles after I thought I was really needing to find one, and when I almost busted into that restroom with my dick feeling damn full of piss, I grabbed it and aimed it for the urinal, and it flew. Well anyway, I guess maybe at that time I was not being real secretive of where the ole piss was coming from. After the first 'bucket full' finally hit the urinal, I kinda stood there and took a deep breath of relief and noticed that two, really good looking, guys were standing there, side by side, and watching everything that was happening. I turned and looked over at 'em and watched one of 'em reaching down and unconsciously grabbing his crotch. Yeah, I will admit I was ready for some action since you and I had not done anything for about three weeks before that, and I just looked at 'em and asked, 'Like it? You like it?'"

"The guy that was grabbing onto his crotch and rubbing it back and forth just said, 'Oh my God Doug – look at that thing, look at it!' Then he looked up at me – I guess to see what I was doing – and then he looked back down at it and asked, 'Can I grab it? Please, can I grab it?' Like I said, I was already horny and wanting some action, so I turned more toward him, took a step closer to him, and said, 'Sure.' I guess right then I really was not concerned if anybody else was going to be coming into the restroom. That just was not on my mind right then. My dick and having someone handle it was one hell of a lot more important right then."

Jim raised up from his licking and nibbling on Chad's ass and simply said, "Keep talking man, keep talking! Listening to you and what in the hell happened in that restroom with those two guys that day is getting me so fucking hot back here that I just might be fucking you with my head in a minute. Come on man, keep it up, cause the more you tell me, the more you are gonna get from me and my tongue back here."

"I pulled it out of my pants farther, he grabbed ahold of it, and of course, you know me, 'hand on my dick, and my dick goes stiff and hard!' I'm standing there in a public restroom with a major boner that I could not have hidden if I had to. The first guy, the one that asked me if he could grab it, grabbed it, jerked and pulled on it and like I said, made it as hard as rock. Then he turned to his buddy and said, 'Grab it man, grab it! It's like grabbing a hot baseball bat. Oh god man, it is so fucking hot!' So then his buddy, who I found out later was his lover, grabbed onto it too. So there I was, kinda out in the public, well in an open restroom anyway, with two guys playing with my rod and jerking on it."

"Oh Chad babe, keep it up, keep it up. You're turning me on man! I'm eating up your ass, so keep up the hot talk! It's making me hungry back here!"

"Yeah man, yeah I can feel it. Chew on my asshole man, chew on it! That is fucking good man, real fucking good. Bite it man, bite on it!"

"I am man, I am! Come on tell me more about you and those guys and what you did. That's making me fucking horny!"

"Okay – okay – chew me – chew me! Yeah, yeah! So anyway, they told me they had a cab-over-camper, out in the parking lot, and they wanted me to go out there with them. Hell man, I was so fucking hot for these two guys right then, there was no way I was gonna turn 'em down. So we went out to the camper and kinda watched that nobody saw all three of us getting in there together, and we got in, and both of 'em started taking my clothes off of me. Within seconds I was in there totally bare assed naked, and offering them one big hard cock. Oh man, they took it. One of 'em, Zack, he got on the end of it and went down on it like a pro and the other one, Doug, he got down under me and ate my balls like they were candy. I had two hot looking guys on me, and under me, and using me for all everything was worth. Pretty soon they both got rid of their clothes and told me to just sit down on Zack's face, and Doug then got up on him and sucked my dick dry. The Zack guy ate my ass just like you're doing right now.

And oh shit man, it felt just as good as my ass is feeling right now! Bite me man – bite it – chew on it!!"

"Hey man, I gotta fuck you, Chad I gotta fuck you!" And with that strong statement, Jim rather jumped up on Chad's back, laid down, pointed his rod at Chad's asshole and poked in. As if he had never fucked this particular asshole before, Jim took it to the extremes! He had Chad's whole body pouncing up and down, with all of the action that he was giving him in the rear.

"Oh my God man, oh my God! Oh shit Jim, that feels fucking good, oh so fucking good. Pound me man, pound me. Beat my ass, beat my ass! Oh Jim I love this, I do!"

"You better baby, cause I am just about to load you with some ole white man cum, and it's cummin now man, it's cummmmmmmin! Oh shit man! Oh shit! I ain't had a cum like that for a hell of a long time. Oh Chad, you telling me about those two guys at the roadside rest I guess must have really turned me on! Oh man, I'm exhausted, I'm fucking exhausted!"

After a few minutes lying there and rather recouping some air and some energy, Chad looked back toward Jim and asked, "Okay man, you just pounded the hell out of me, now you ready to get pounded?"

"Oh hell no man, I can't. Honestly Chad, today is maybe the only day in your life that you get fucked and don't fuck some guy back, but today all I wanted was to fuck you and let you be the good guy down below and taking it from above. You remember you told me one day that you were always the one doing the fucking and nobody ever lets you be the bottom guy? Well today, you are just the bottom guy. I'll get you back up in my butt the next time, but for today, it's all about you and your ass! And thanks man, thanks!"

"Hey thanks man, but I'll fuck you if you want. Seriously man, you want me to fuck you?"

"No Chad, no. I mean it man, I wanted us to get together today just so I could take care of that hot ass you've got. I got to lie there, and chew and nibble on that ass like it was some kind of a chocolate Sundae, with nuts on it, and then I got to pound the hell out of it and give you the same ass action that I get from you so often, so no, today it's just your ass, and not mine. But thanks man, thanks. We'll get together later this week and then I'll let you pound me like you were trying to chop down some big old Sequoia tree."

"Hey thanks man, thanks. Honestly, I've never been treated so nice. Yeah, gotta admit I sure do love poking some guy's ass, and especially yours, but for you to treat me this way, it's great!"

"Okay man, let's see if you can finish up telling me about you and those two guys on your way to Detroit, that is, without me getting so hot and horny over listening to it that I just gotta climb all over you and get stuff started all over again."

"Well, that was kind of the end of it once I sat down on Zack's face and he ate my ass like there was no tomorrow, and Doug tried to make his throat bigger and bigger by pushing more of my dick down in it than there was room for. Doug sucked me hard enough, though, to where I loaded his guts with some good old black man cum – like I had not dropped into some guy's mouth for quite a while."

"This all happened in their camper, there in the parking area?"

"Yeah, yeah. We had to kind of try to keep everything on the quiet side, and also not rock the camper too much since there were other people close by. The window blinds were of course closed, but one of them would peek out every once in a while to make sure we weren't attracting too much attention. So anyway, things were pretty calm then, but the next night at their house, things were kinda different."

"The next night at their house!!?? You went to their house?"

"Yeah, I was headed for Detroit and that's where they live, so they wanted me to come to their place if I could, and wanting to fuck both of those asses – I made time to do it. Two hot tight asses like theirs, I needed that, and they needed it too."

"So like how old are these guys?"

"Both right at twenty five or twenty six. Both former football players in high school, and now both of 'em have jobs that really keeps 'em in shape. Zack is a personal trainer, and Doug runs a health club, so you can imagine how both of 'em are built and how they look."

"So, at their house. What happened?"

"I fucked each of them, while his partner ate my ass out – well as much as he could since I kept moving my ass up and down – then they each used my ass for some "physical training," and what I found rather unusual was the way they liked to have their tits bitten as much and as often as possible. And I don't mean just kinda bitten, I mean really bitten. They told me that was the reason that they ended up together. Some other guy knew both of them, but they did not yet know each other, and so this other guy got them together since he knew they both liked the tit biting thing, and they said it was history from then. They found each other, they liked each other, they liked the way each other played, and it went from there. Said they've been together now for four years."

"So I assume now that you will be going back to see them again when you do a trip to Detroit, right?"

"Right! Damn right I am, and it better be pretty damn soon!"

———————

"Hey Chad. Everything okay? You've been kinda on the quiet side lately, everything okay?"

"Well yes and no. Judy and I are gonna be splitting."

"What!? Why? What happened man? What happened?"

"I took a phone call a few days ago that I shouldn't have. One of my guys in Detroit called me to see when I was gonna be in Detroit next time, and that kinda started everything. I guess maybe she had been wondering about what all I was doing on my out of town trips, and so the questions just kept coming and coming. She told me that she figured I was probably fucking with some gals, and I kept telling her, "No, I am not!" So then she finally just laid it on the line and asked me if I was fucking around with guys and I had to finally just tell her, 'Yes.' I had to level with her and quit my lying to her all of the time. She told me that she had been wondering for a long time now because of the way I was acting around her, and not being very anxious for sex when she thought I should be real horny and anxious, and I was not. She wants a divorce. And yeah, I will be honest and tell you that yes, I want a divorce too, but going through that is gonna be a big pile of shit."

"Uh, Chad. She know anything about us? Your in-town activities?"

"No, no! No – don't be worried about that. That's not even on the table for conversation. She's not gonna know anything about that, she's just all pissed because I've been playing with the Detroit guys. I knew when I gave Doug my number, that I probably shouldn't have, but honestly, at that time, I really did not care."

"So Chad, what's happening with you and those Detroit guys? You been able to see them pretty often? You getting up there a lot?"

"Yeah, some truck trips, and over the last few months, I've taken a few week-end days and made a fast run up there, and I know that is how Judy kinda got suspicious of what was going on. I wasn't making very good excuses of why I had to be 'out on the road' when I was sneaking in those extra trips, and she got smart."

"Oh shit Chad, I don't know what to say. I'm sorry, I guess. But you admitted that you wanted the divorce too, so maybe it is best for you. So what's gonna happen now? What you gonna do?"

"I'm turning in my two weeks' notice today, and just as soon as the two weeks are up, I'm headed for Detroit. I've already called Doug and Zack – told them what happened – and we're following through on some talks that we've had the last few times I've been up there, and that is, we're setting up a three-sum. We all want to live together, take each other as a husband, do things for each other, help each other any way we can, and just plain live and enjoy life as a loving three-sum of guys. Three guys, one house, one love and three very happy guys, living life free and carefree. We've talked about this for some time now – every time I go up there – and we had already decided that if something like this did happen, then I was going to quit my job down here, move up there, and we are gonna become a three-sum 'couple.' All three of us together. All of us get along so well, we all love each other, we all kinda like the same stuff, we all like the way we each like to play in bed, and I gotta tell you, as a three-sum, the sex is out of this world! And so for some time now, we've all been kind of looking forward to this, and so now it's gonna happen. I talked to the guys this morning, and we've all agreed, it's time! So Jim, I sure have enjoyed our time together, and I sure have enjoyed our playing together, but the time has come. We've got two more weeks available to do some of our fun stuff, then I'm off to Detroit, and my two new husbands. I'm finally gonna be true to myself, and live the type of life I'm supposed to. I'm finally gonna be doing my preferred thing, and doing it every night."

"Oh Chad, what can I say? On one hand I am so glad for you, but on the other hand, I feel like I'm losing one very good and close friend. Our friendship, the public, and the private friendship, are both so important to me that I hate to know that they are coming to an end. Chad, you are one lucky guy though. Two men to love you! And two men for you to love! Chad, it really can't get any better than that!"

"You are right! You've sure made my days and nights a hell of a lot better ever since you followed me into that restroom that day, and insisted on playing with my rod, and I've appreciated each and every time we've done stuff together since then. Jim, truly I am going to miss you. I've told Doug and Zack all about you and our friendship, and of course our playing with each other, and they told me to let you know that they will be taking damn good care of 'your' man when I get up there. If Doug's not home, then Zack'll be there, and if Zack's not there, then Doug'll be home, and hey, if I'm not there, then those two can act like it was one of their old days, before big ole Chad showed up! Jim, thanks for being you, and thanks for insisting that first day that we get it on and do some stuff. All of the stuff has been great fun."

"Chad, it's been more than fun, it's been great. Now, all I can hope is that I will be able to find me a replacement that is as great of a guy, as you are, and have been. Yeah Chad, you got one hell of a hot body on you, but you've got a mind and a personality that completely overshadows that body. Chad, I am jealous of what you are headed for, and I hope you the best, and I wish you the best, and I hope you never forget all of the great times you and I have had together. Chad, you are my man!" And with one great big smile on his face, Jim grabbed Chad, pulled him forward and actually gave him a bigger and a stronger hug, than he had ever done before.

Chad hugged back, stepped back a step, looked at Jim, smiled, and then said, "Well, I guess it is gonna take two men, to replace you, ain't it?"

Black Jerry's Moving Day

Chapter One: In The Mirror

Tom had just left his house, after about three hours of being on the computer reading gay Erotic stories, and of course, since he refers to himself as *'the little, pale face, white guy,'* he definitely prefers reading the interracial stories first. He has been very fortunate – using his terminology – of having had some very exciting gay sexual activities with a number of black men in the past, and he knew without question that he was a true active member of the statement, 'If you go Black, you never go back!'

Of course, Tom did not turn down the opportunity of fooling around with white guys either, but if he ever had the situation happen when he had to decide between the choice of white or black, he knew there would be no choice to make. To him it's – 'Black is real tight – Black is real right!'

Well, as he was now headed down Main Street, only about five or ten minutes after he finally pulled himself away from his, 'White man gets fucked by the big muscular black hunk' stories, he just got a glimpse of what he thought had to be coming straight out of one of his interracial stories, that he had just been drooling all over – just minutes earlier.

As he was sitting at the traffic light at Main and Silver, a "You Move Yourself" rental truck pulled up beside him, and for only one slight moment, he got transformed from reality, to becoming one of the main characters, in one of his stories. One of the characters, that just happens to see a beautiful hot black body, that he just has to get to, somehow!

As the truck pulled up beside him on the passenger side of his car, he turned and so very quickly saw what looked like to him, to be absolutely the most beautiful, of all black men. He managed to move his car just enough so that he could see his "God of the moment," in the rear view mirror on the truck. As he was admiring the small part of his man that he could see in the mirror, the driver looked back at him, through the mirror, and Tom did know that he had definitely been caught checking out this driver!

The driver smiled, so very slightly nodded, and then drove on as the light changed. Tom's nervous system took a major, major leap in excitement. For three or four more traffic lights, this same occurrence transpired. Tom would pull up just slightly behind the truck and get himself positioned just right so that he could admire the driver and allow his inner thoughts to play tricks on what he would love to be doing right then, instead of driving around town, in a car.

Tom was no way out of his way, from where he originally was headed for. That original destination was now of no importance, if he could continue, even for a very short time longer, his not so secret admiration of this unknown driver.

After each traffic stop, Tom always made sure that he allowed the truck to proceed in front of him so that he could maintain control of how to come up beside or just to the rear of the truck and get his viewing position. At each light, the truck driver would look back at him through the mirror and give him an ever so slight of a grin. The driver was obviously enjoying this attention, and the obvious admiration that he was the center of.

Going through the most recent traffic light, the truck moved to the right lane, as Tom then did also, but that was still to the lane beside the truck. As the truck turned into a restaurant parking lot, Tom was in the wrong lane to also turn, so his immediate reaction was to quickly get into the far right lane, and turn into the next exit and come back toward the restaurant. He knew that if that driver was as aware of just what was happening, and Tom was just sure he was, he would see Tom coming back toward the restaurant through the parking lot. Tom's anxiety level simply went out of the roof. He simply knew (oh God he was praying) that the driver was of the attitude to meet his private admirer, and he was using the restaurant as the common meeting grounds for them to use. Tom was determined to help that driver with his aims and projections. Tom pulled into the restaurant parking lot with his chest and his heart pounding loudly. He knew his hormones were getting way out of control. The amount of time on the computer reading about little white guys, and the fun that they had been having with some big, strong, good looking, and well hung black men, seemed to possibly becoming, a true reality for him. No fiction story here, he thought. This is the real thing!

As he casually got out of his car, he locked the door, turned to walk toward the restaurant and much to his shock, he suddenly realized that his big black hunk of a playmate, (well so he was hoping, anyway), was assisting a lady out of the passenger side of the truck. Never in this whole drive and chase, had he been able to see into the passenger side of the truck, and in his complete involvement of admiring the stud of a driver, did he even ponder the possibility that somebody else just might be in the truck with him! That possibility just never occurred to him! That thought never entered his mind! He was simply way too hung up in the dream of getting to know this man, that no stumbling block – like maybe a wife – could be possible.

Well, now being in the parking lot, having gotten out of his car and having locked the doors of it, he did feel rather compelled to go ahead and go into the restaurant so that he did not come across as some kind of an "out of his mind" goofy character. He knew his hot driver had seen him rather retreat, back to the restaurant from the farther entrance.

Right then the only thing that Tom could think, was, "I'm making a damn fool out of myself," and also, "Damn it, he kept looking back at me in the mirror! And when he did, he grinned! I wonder if he was thinking of me as some complete ass of a fool? I wonder if he thinks I am really some weird, 'off of the wall,' type of a guy? Damn man! Shit! I was really wanting to try and meet this guy!"

Tom entered the restaurant before his 'man of the day' – his 'dream man of his life' – and the lady entered. Tom took a small two-person booth just shortly inside of the front door. He seated himself so that he would be looking toward the door, and toward most of the tables and booths.

As he was getting himself all positioned in the booth, the hunk and the lady came in. His hunk, as he was now internally thinking of him, let the lady precede him into the restaurant, and as they walked past Tom, the hunk looked down at Tom and, with a very slight and very pleasant grin on his face, he nodded. His position of being behind the lady prevented her from seeing what had just happened and transpired.

Now Tom was real confused. "Damn! Did he grin and nod at me because he might maybe want to meet me, like I want to meet him, or is he internally laughing at me for being such a complete fool out on the street in tracking and following him?"

Right then he was truly wishing that he could find out if, or if not, he and his rather tracking actions out on the street had been mentioned to the lady that was in the truck, or had his actions been kept a total secret?

As Tom turned sideways to kind of lean up against the wall and the booth back at the same time, he realized that his object of attraction had taken a booth just to the right of him, and there was one empty booth between them. As he casually glanced to his right as if to look for a waitress, he did notice that his big strong black male hunk was seated so that he could see Tom. His lady was facing the opposite direction. Tom did hear her ask, "Jerry, why are we getting something to eat now? It's going to be lunch time pretty soon, and if we eat now, we won't want any lunch. I really don't understand why you think you need something now!"

"Hey Hon," the hunky muscle man replied. "I've been loading that damn truck all morning long, and as soon as we get it over to Simpson Street, I will be unloading it all afternoon, and I just plain want something in my stomach now. OK?"

Tom heard it all. Yeah, he heard it, and he kind of liked what he heard! This food stop was not planned. They were local people, and they were not leaving town. They were just headed for Simpson Street, and then he would be unloading the truck! Yeah – he heard the word "Hon" too, so he had to assume that lady, was the lucky one of the day, being the one person that got to snuggle up close to that body of God, each night in bed! He had to now assume, that the hunk of a man that he had been drooling over, was her husband.

As Tom rather raised his hand to gain the attention of a waitress, he could see from the corner of his eye that "Mr. Hunk" was looking past the lady across the table from him, and was looking directly toward Tom. This simply made Tom's dick flick and flutter. Some of his earlier thoughts, the ones he had before he found out that there was a lady in the truck also, were returning.

The waitress stopped at Mr. Hunk's table and took their order. Tom heard the order, two complete breakfasts, eggs, bacon, hash browns and the whole thing. Oh, he thought, this is not going to be a fast in and a fast out meal! The hunk is playing it slowly. Tom had to wonder if that was on purpose, or was he really that hungry at this time of day?

After getting the order at the Mr. Hunk and his lady's table, the waitress then approached Tom's table and took his order. All of a sudden, Tom had decided that he too needed a little more than just a cup of coffee. Looking at the menu again, Tom decided on bacon and eggs also. Similar meal, should take a very similar amount of time to be prepared.

As Tom rather settled back and attempted to pay attention to some of the artwork on the walls, and waiting on his order, he continued to keep his ears open for any new and exciting comments that he just might happen to hear. He was still in the mental process stages of hoping that Mr. Hunk was actually trying to find a way to meet him, but in a very secret, and devious way, of course.

He overheard the big, muscular, hunky, black man making some rather negative comments about how full that truck was, and how getting it unloaded was going to be a real time taker, and how he now wished that he had hired someone to help.

"You know Hon," he said, "by the time we get this damn truck all unloaded, it is going to be too late to get it back to the rental company, and I am then going to have to pay for an entire day's rental on it. That is going to be probably another fifty or sixty bucks, and I wish now I was paying that money to someone,

someone to help me, rather than to the rental company and getting nothing for it."

"Jerry," his lady said. "I tried to tell you a few days ago that I thought you might need some help, but you kept telling me that you could do it all by yourself. If you want to see if you can find someone now, it's kind of at the last minute, but I still do think you ought to have some help." Tom now knew that the hunk's name was Jerry! Mentally he really could not keep from running the words, 'Oh how I want to marry Jerry – oh how I want to marry Jerry,' through his mind!

"Hey Hon, while we wait on our meals, I'm going to ask around and see if anyone here knows of somebody that might be available for an afternoon of work. Hey, let me ask that guy that came in right before we did. He might be local and know of someone!"

Jerry got up from the table and approached Tom's table.

"Hi guy. My name is Jerry. Julie, my wife, and I are in the process of moving from one side of town to the other, and I was kind of foolish in thinking that I could do everything all by myself, and now I do realize that I was kind of wrong. Do you happen to know of anybody that might be interested in making about fifty bucks this afternoon and helping me get the truck unloaded over on Simpson Street, real close to the intersection of Wilson St.?" Jerry asked, as he spread a very large grin across his face as he talked to Tom.

"Yeah – uh yeah. I'm just goofing the day off," Tom replied. "I was going to go meet up with a friend and just kind of hang out with him this afternoon, but yeah – yeah – I could use the bucks, and sure, I'm available if you think I might work out for you!"

Tom returned the grin, and in fact, a much larger grin than had been offered to him.

"Oh, my name is Tom! I'll need to run past my place and get some other clothes on first though, if I can. I live pretty close to here, so doing that won't take me too long. Where do I meet you, and when should I be there?"

Jerry asked the waitress for a piece of paper, and he then said, "Hey Tom, let me give you the address, and as soon as we eat, we'll be headed over there ourselves."

Jerry sat down across the table from Tom to write down the address, and he also gave him a cell phone number so that he would have it if necessary. Tom, in return, also gave Jerry his own cell phone number, for hopefully more than one reason, and very excitedly noticed that as Jerry sat across the table from him, writing down the address, Jerry was rubbing the side of Tom's leg, with his own. Tom looked at Jerry once immediately following one of the more forceful rubs, and Jerry just slightly shook his head in an affirmative motion, looked at Tom, and smiled. Tom's heart started pounding! He simply knew that this was a guy-to-guy, come on. He knew Jerry was really saying, "Hey man, I want you, and I want to play with you!" He looked at Jerry, grinned and smiled. He smiled big!

Jerry got up, put his right hand on Tom's shoulder and said, "Well man, I'm certainly glad that you just happened to be in here at the same time we were. I sure am going to enjoy using your help this afternoon. I did not think it would be so easy for me to find someone for this afternoon. But, hey man, if you don't mind getting a little hot and sweaty, I'm sure glad you are going to be working with me. We'll see you over there shortly. OK?"

"Yeah, great!" Tom replied, as he looked up at what had suddenly become one of the most beautiful faces that he had ever seen in his entire life. He returned a very large smile to Jerry and said, "I'll eat, go grab some more suitable clothes and see you over there! I'm glad I can help, man!"

Jerry returned to his own table and told Julie that finding someone was much easier than he had thought it would be. He told her that the guy behind her was available and was going to be helping him out.

As Tom heard Jerry tell Julie, "and was going to be helping him out," Tom immediately thought, "Oh yeah man! And he is going to be helping me out too, if everything works out the way that it looks like I and Jerry, both, are looking forward to. Tom especially liked Jerry's comment about getting all hot and sweaty. Yeah – hot and sweaty, but not from just unloading the truck. It might be from some really funny, good, active hands on stuff that just might happen, while they're up in the truck getting it unloaded, or at least trying to get it unloaded.

After all, ordering the more complete meal, the one that takes longer to get fixed, turned out to be unnecessary, but realizing that he was going to be doing a little more active work this afternoon than he had originally planned on, Tom was glad that he was getting a bigger meal. As he finished his meal, he went to Jerry's table and told him that he would meet them at the house address just as soon as he grabbed some other clothes. While at the table, he met Julie and told her that he was glad that he was available that afternoon, and that he was glad that he would be able to help them get moved into their new house.

Tom excused himself, paid for his meal, waved back toward Jerry, smiled, and headed out the door and to his house.

As he got to the house, he thought, "Clothes – clothes! Oh man, what in the hell am I going to wear this afternoon? I've got to have something that looks pretty respectful, but also something that will make me look as hot and as sexy and attractive as possible. No underwear, I know that! So – some shorts that are not too short. I don't want my dick hanging out at the wrong times, but yet something that is hot looking. Tank top! Yeah – I've got to show off my body as much as possible. I wanna look real hot for Jerry! I want him to know I'm trying to look real hot for him!'

Tom selected his wardrobe for the afternoon, and in addition, grabbed an extra change of more respectful clothes, just in case he needed something for after they got the truck done. As he was gathering things together, he mentally started the very happy thoughts of just thinking what he and Jerry could, or would, look like having sex together.

"What a sight – what a good hot and hunky sight," Tom thought! "Me, five foot nine, a hundred and eighty five pounds, tight gym constructed built, blond hair and my pale white skin. It kind of looks like, to me anyway, that Jerry is pretty close to my age, twenty-eight, but other than that, not a hell of a lot of similarity between us. First thing, he is of course the most beautiful shade of mahogany that any man has probably ever been, probably right at about six foot tall, probably weighs in at about two twenty or two twenty five and from the sight of those arms and that chest sticking out from that t-shirt, damn man – damn man – one hell of a hot, strong, muscular body on him. Total power man, a total power. I wonder if he was a college wrestler or some competition bodybuilder or just why he is built so damn hot? Right now, all I can do is imagine just what kind of a big long black meat steak he is hanging between those power legs of his. I am sure it will probably be one of, if not the greatest, that I have ever had the pleasure of seeing, touching, or getting either in my mouth, or up in my ass. That is – if everything goes just right, and I am not mentally over imaging everything that I think is going on! Oh if everything goes right, I'm sure my dick is not going to compare to his, but damn I do have to admit that even a number of the black men that I have had the pleasure of sexing around with have all been very complementary about it. For hanging from a pale white guy, it hangs farther, and when stiff, sticks out farther than just about any other white dicks. How and why I got what I got, I do not know, but I sure am thankful for it, and I've made a few other guys thankful for it too."

"Shit man, all I can say right now is that if I have really misunderstood his smiles, his grins, his fancy way of getting to meet me and have me work with him, and especially the ole, 'under the table,' leg rubs, if I am wrong, I am going to be one sorry little crying sobbing kid tonight! Shit man! I hope to hell I did not read stuff into this that really is not there. Come to think about it, this is way too much like a porno video, when everything just happens to work out so automatically and nothing gets in the way of some hot guy getting in the pants, and usually the ass hole, of some other hot hunk. Those porno videos are so fake! Hell nothing, and I do mean nothing, ever goes wrong for those hungry, horny, ass hungry, cock sucking, ass sucking and ball-chewing guys. Shit man! Today is working out way too close to one of those movies. Shit man, this had better not go wrong! When a man sits across the table from you and secretly rubs his leg up against yours and then grins at you, there can't be any other meaning to it than –'let's fuck man!' Is there?"

Tom threw his extra clothes in the back seat of his car and headed out for Jerry and Julie's new home. He was real anxious to get to that address.

Oh yeah – he also realized that he was also getting real anxious to help Jerry carry his bed in. Yeah, he knew, there was a gal for in that bed too, but just the mental picture of Jerry in that bed, screwing anybody, man or woman, was a damn hot picture for him to imagine! Right now he just got all excited knowing that soon he would be able to get his hands on the very mattress that Jerry puts his bare butt on, and if everything works out the right way, he will be able to put his face up against that mattress and let Jerry see him caressing the space where he lays his bare butt each night. Oh, what a great thought! "I never thought I would get so excited about just putting my face on a mattress just because it is the mattress of some special person. Hell man, if I get a chance, I'll lick that mattress as I help Jerry carry it in. And if possible, I'll make sure Jerry sees me licking it! I'll ask him what side of the bed he sleeps on, and then lick it again."

Tom got to the house, and got out of his car just as Jerry came around from the other side of the truck. "Oh shit, oh shit!" Was just about all he could think at the time. Jerry had been to the house long enough to dump the Levi's for a cooler, shorter, tighter and definitely sexier pair of gym shorts. A pair that was definitely showing a very nicely shaped basket. Tom's mouth hung open and he continued to take deep breaths of air. Jerry looked at him, and quietly asked, "Like it? Like what you see? I changed for you!"

The chest was a monument to the well-built man, and the legs were true tree trunks meant for the national forests someplace. Jerry knew he was now on display, and Tom was now totally convinced that the leg rubbing in the restaurant was no accident.

As Tom glanced around to make sure nobody else, especially Julie, was within ear shot, he replied, "Oh man, oh man. Like it? Oh shit man, oh shit! Oh God Jerry, I hope like hell you are not trying to play with my mind!"

"Hell no man – no I'm not! Not your mind man, but I see some other parts of your body that I want to get my hands on just as soon as we get that truck emptied enough where I can do some good ole playing around up in the far end of it." Then looking around left and right to make sure the hedge hid them completely, Jerry reached out, took management of Tom's crotch – like grabbing onto and controlling some part of a company – and said, "Come on man, let's see how fast we can get ourselves a little play space made up in that truck!"

Chapter Two: I Gotta See This Thing!

Jerry unlocked and swung open the back doors, and as he got the left door standing open between himself and the house, he then leaned over toward Tom and softly said, "Hey, we need to work up some hot sweat here pretty quickly so that we'll have a good reason to pull our shirts off and not look like maybe we're doing it needlessly. I can see those nipples of yours sticking out, and just as soon as we can, I wanna see if I can suck some milk out of one of 'em."

Standing there in an almost complete shock, all Tom could utter was a low, "Oh man, oh man! Oh Jerry, you mean it, you mean it?"

Continuing to stand there with the door only partly swung back, Jerry looked at Tom and as he reached up and pinched Tom's left tit, he soundly stated, "Oh hell yes man, hell yes!" When you got out of your car at the restaurant, I knew then that I had not made a mistake deciding that I needed something to eat, and now I know damn well what it is that I want to chew on."

With that statement being stated, Jerry then opened the door the rest of the way, folded it against the side of the truck, then opened the right door, and as he finished folding it up against the side of the truck, took a quick look toward the house and then 'instructed' Tom to climb up into the truck. Wondering just why Jerry was now giving such specific instructions, Tom did step over to the middle of the open truck and started to lift his leg up to step on the bumper of the truck, and as he did, suddenly he realized that Jerry had very firmly placed his hand right in the crack of Tom's ass and with one strong and quick movement, he had completely lifted Tom up and into the truck.

Landing on his hands and knees, Tom quickly turned around to face Jerry, and with one very big grin on his face, he simply said, "Thank you! Thank you!"

Standing on the ground, at the back of the truck bed, and with a very big grin on his face too, he looked up at Tom and said, "God man, you got one hot, tight, solid ass! Damn I'm glad I did that."

Jerry then climbed up into the truck and as if necessary to help himself stand up, he grabbed Tom's crotch and just said, "Thanks." Then for just a few moments, Jerry did stand there and tell Tom that when he backed the truck in, be parked it so that it did not open directly at the front door nor at a window, and that he suggested that while they were up in the truck together, that they do try diligently, to keep an ear open for either Julie or maybe some neighbor to come walking up to the door unexpectedly. He also mentioned that what his 'plan' was to get some of the smaller stuff out of the truck, then slide the tall bookcase over and let it create somewhat of a sight barrier, so that they could once in a while maybe reach over and feel some major part of the other guy. Tom grinned, and then told Jerry, "Hey man, I wanna feel EVERY part of you, not just a major part." Jerry grinned back and said, "Ditto!"

After some rather 'required' touching and feeling of each other when they could manage to be in a more secure spot, they did manage to start getting some of the cargo (household items) removed from the truck and into the house. Quite occasionally they would manage to find themselves in a position where one man needed to squeeze past the other man, and in the process just happen to make some friendly body contact with the other individual. These contacts did happen just after one of the horny men confirmed that Julie was securely placed, in perhaps the kitchen, putting something in the cupboards. More than once it just so happened that Jerry would suggest to Tom that he, "Take this box up to the master bedroom, and put it in the closet."

For some very unexplained reason, Jerry too would then just happen to have another box that also needed to be placed in the same closet, and needless to say, as Tom was sitting his box down, for some 'mysterious reason,' Jerry would 'just happen to be there,' with his box, and of course manage to block Tom's way out of the closet – that is until Jerry had very successfully felt down into either the front, or the rear, of Tom's shorts.

During one of the upstairs bedroom closet encounters, it was the first time that Jerry explored the front of Tom's shorts, and he almost let out a shocking explanation, a little too loudly, as he strongly stated, "Oh my God man! What in the hell are you hiding in there? I've grabbed this crotch a couple of times and it sure never felt like what I've got in my hand on now! Tom, this is enormous! It's enormous! Come on man, we gotta take some stuff down into the basement. I gotta see this thing!"

"Well Jerry, it's okay, but I'm sure yours has got to be a lot bigger than mine. All afternoon I've been afraid to do, to you, what you're doing right now. I've been afraid that Julie might come walking in, but I gotta see yours man, I gotta. You got stuff that needs to go to the basement?"

"Yeah, yeah I do. It's still up in the front end of the truck, but we can get to it so we can go down to the basement. There's a back storage room down there, so we can kinda use it for a second or two and let you see mine, and then I can pull your shorts down and take a good long look at this log. Come on, lets get some stuff out of the truck."

As Jerry and Tom got back up into the truck to get some of the stuff that needed to be taken to the basement, Tom saw some new sides of Jerry's life that he had not even asked about.

"Oh hey! Kids bicycles. Jerry you got kids?"

"Oh yeah. Two. One girl aged eight and a boy four. Guess I never mentioned them did I? They're at Grandma's house today. Julie and I did not think we needed them running around while we are trying to get stuff done. Their bedroom stuff is up on the front of the load, so we haven't gotten to it yet. If we had, then I'm sure you would have figured out that kids are part of the family."

"Oh weights! And a weight lifting bench. Okay, now I know for damn sure why you are built like one of those big Caterpillar underground mining drills. The kind that drills tunnels. I saw a picture of one of them one day, and I swear you are built just as strong as one of them monster machines. When I saw that machine, I never thought I'd associate it with some sexy hot built man, but right now, that's about the only way I can think of you and that body of yours. Now, when I see a Caterpillar tractor working out on the road someplace, I'm gonna think of you and wish I had you there pushing me around like they push the ground around. I just got me a whole new respect for those big strong Caterpillar tractors. Every time I see one of them, I'm gonna call it my, 'Jerry Machine.'"

"Yeah, this is some of the stuff that needs to go to the basement. Feel up to helping me get these weights down to the basement?"

"Yes, hell yes. Especially if we get to do what you mentioned a little bit ago."

"Okay let's do it. I'm not planning on taking all of the weights all at once, too damn much for what you're calling a Caterpillar tractor, so since we're gonna have to make a number of trips back and forth, that'll give us a little more of a chance to grab each other, okay?"

"Hell yes, okay!" Tom stated firmly. "Come on man, let's do it. I wanna see what you're hiding down there. And down there, I don't mean in the basement, I mean in those shorts with that big bulge showing. I've been wanting to see that thing ever since I first saw you earlier today, and now I'm gonna. Let's go, let's do it!"

"Hey wait! Before we start taking this stuff to the basement, let's go in and tell Julie that we're hot and thirsty and we need a couple of beers, and then, since we're so hot, it'll be a good time to strip out of our shirts. Okay?"

"Yeah, but let me tell you something man. When you take that shirt off, don't be surprised if I just fucking faint right there on the floor. Seriously Jerry, I've never been around some guy that is as hot as you are, so keep me under control when I see that chest – all hot and bare!"

Jerry and Tom did go into the house and grabbed a couple of beers, and told Julie that they were going to start taking the weights and the other workout equipment down to the basement, and then finish up bringing in the other furniture. Julie then told them that she had just talked to her Mom on the phone, and that she was going to run over to her Mom's house for a few minutes to help her Mom fix supper for the kids. She then added, "I need a small break from all of this packing and unpacking."

Jerry asked her to stop at a store and buy some more beer, since he now had a helper to share the beer with, and how he was now not, the only beer guzzler in the house.

Jerry and Julie had two cars, and they had previously brought her car on over, to the new address, and Jerry's was at the truck rental location.

As she left the house, there was no longer the four or five feet separation between Jerry and Tom. Immediately Tom sat his beer down on the counter, and grabbed Jerry in each and every spot that he could grab onto. Jerry returned the 'favor.' Just as quickly as he possibly could, Jerry opened the button to Tom's shorts, pulled them down, and shockingly said, "Oh! No briefs or under shorts, uh? My – my! I wondered why I didn't feel any underwear. I would kinda guess then, that someone in here was hoping that maybe his shorts would be taken down, and he sure didn't want any underwear getting in the way. Right? I was right wasn't I? That's one hell of a nice big rod you're carry around in those shorts, ain't it? Damn good thing it never got hard while Julie was still here, or she would have been looking at about half of it sticking out the bottom of those shorts. You weren't no dummy at the restaurant were you? You knew what was going on, and you wanted to be ready for it, didn't you?"

"You are right!" Tom excitedly answered. "Oh Jerry, I can't believe that I've got my dick out and you're grabbing it. Oh man, I've been praying for this ever since I saw you in the truck. Oh Jerry, get yours out! Oh Jerry, let me have yours. I gotta see yours!"

And with that request for action, Jerry did pull off his t-shirt, and then did drop his shorts. Fortunately before Julie had left, his pole was not showing any excitement, but it sure was now! A full eleven inches of excitement! Stiff, warm, hard blood rushing excitement!

"Oh my God, oh my God!" Tom exclaimed in shocked amazement. "Oh Jerry, oh man it is so fucking big! Oh man, can you fuck guys with that thing?"

"Oh yeah, oh yeah. Yeah, I fuck 'em and fuck 'em until they finally tell me that they just can't take any more. It's the guys that first look at it and then want to run, that turn out being the ones that don't want to quit, once I get it up in their butts and I've shot off. What's your reaction Tom – like it? Anxious for it, or afraid of it? Wanting to pull your shorts back up and cover up that big boner you got and run, or are you now wanting to see what a big woody pushed up in your ass feels like, so you'll know what your bottom boys are feeling when you're sticking that big boner of yours up in 'em?"

"Oh yeah man, I want that, I really do. Jerry, I gotta suck on it and then I want you to put it up in my ass for a second or two. I know we gotta keep getting the stuff off of the truck, but please, I wanna taste it and then I want you to put some cream or something in my ass, and just push it up in there for a minute."

"Okay, suck on it for a minute. But just for a minute, cause we gotta keep working, and then we're gonna go in the bathroom and one quick in and back out. Okay? I wanna do more with you, but we gotta get that truck done, and besides I don't want Julie coming home and finding us fucking each other. Understand?"

"Oh yeah man, oh yeah! I understand," Tom stated as he immediately took the entire eleven inches down into his throat."

"Oh shit man! Damn you are one hell of a cocksucker, aren't you? Seriously man, I don't remember any other guy that ever went down on my cock as fucking fast as you did! Shit man, you just opened up your mouth and took the whole thing all at once. Wow! Shocked me! Okay, now off of it, and into the bathroom. Now I'm anxious to see if you can take it up the ass as fast as you took it down the throat!"

About one minute later, and in the bathroom, Jerry grabbed some hand cream – that was in a moving box on the floor – he dabbed some on Tom's bare ass that was sticking out, as he leaned on the lavatory edge, turned, grabbed his rod, aimed it, and with one push drove it to the bottom of Tom's hole.

"Oh my God man, you took the whole fucking thing in one push! Tom, you took my whole dick in one push man – one push! Nobody has ever done that before. Shit man, you okay? Seriously Tom, is your ass okay? Nobody has ever taken that dick that fast. I thought I was gonna make you kinda yell some and then maybe ask me to go slower, but shit man – you took it like it was some train headed into a tunnel! Damn man, I can't believe it! Do you get fucked a lot? How long you been getting it in the ass?"

"Oh God, that felt good! Oh Jerry, that was great! Oh, I get fucked probably three or four times a month. I've been getting fucked ever since I moved back here from Kansas City about four years ago. I got a buddy by the name of Dean that's got a good sized poker on him, not as big as yours, but a good size and he does me at least three or four times a month. But today, I just knew that if you were gonna ram me, I really wanted to be all good and ready, and I just managed to make my ass hole relax so that I could take it as fast as possible, and oh thank God, I did. Oh Jerry, it feels so good up in there."

"Yeah I know it probably does, and my dick feels good stuffed up in there, but like I told you, it was gonna be just one shove up and in there, then I gotta pull it out so we can get some work done. I wanna do this some more, but now is not the time. I gotta pull me back out and we gotta get some of this stuff unloaded, or Julie is gonna be asking what in the hell we did while she was gone." He pulled his rod, back out.

"Hey Jerry, you got any underwear that I can put on? Some tight briefs kind? Since it's just you and me here right now, I'd love to put on a pair of your underwear and wear them the rest of the day. Just the idea of knowing that I've got your underwear on and I'm still here helping you unload the truck, oh that makes me feel so horny. I'll be able to rub my crotch and know that what I am rubbing up against me and my dick, is the same underwear that you've had on your crotch, and you've had it rubbing and grabbing onto you and your dick. And when Julie gets back, I'll know I've got your underwear on, and it's holding my dick up and in place like it has yours, and she won't know it! Oh man, you got any I can put on?"

"Yeah, I've got some. Fact is, here take these, the ones I've got on right now. Then some of my flaky skin that has rubbed off in 'em will maybe stick to you. Want these?"

"Oh shit yes man, hell yes! Yeah man, yeah man. A pair that you've been hiding your dick and your butt in – oh man, what a fucking turn on!"

As Jerry did pull it back out, he then pulled his underwear off, handed them to Tom, and told him that he was gonna go see if he could find some, that maybe Julie had already put in the dresser, but if not, he'd just go without any since Julie didn't know anyway if he had put briefs on that day or not. He told Tom that he often does not wear any, anyway, so if he couldn't find any, no big deal. He then said, "Hey, tell you what. I gotta take the truck back and get my car, and besides I gotta stop by an ATM and get the cash I owe you, so when we're done, when I ask if you wanna follow me to the truck spot, you agree. Okay? You said you live by yourself over on Bradley, right? Can we stop in there for just a few minutes after we drop off the truck, and then let me have about five minutes up in that hot, tight, little, white ass of yours?"

"Oh God yes. Oh hell yes we can. Yeah, let's do that."

And with those 'pre-planned' moments of fucking Tom's ass again – all rather pre-scheduled – and after Jerry did find a pair of underwear to put on, the two did get back to unloading the truck, and moving the weights down to the basement. Of course it did take about twice as long to get them down there, since for some very funny reason, every time Tom got close to Jerry, or Jerry got close to Tom, somebody's hand did, for some unexplainable reason, reach out and always manage to grab onto a nice hunk of meat, that just happened to be hiding neatly between the man's legs.

For just about another two hours, the two hot and horny guys did manage to continue unloading the truck, and did manage, very secretively, to take every possible opportunity to feel an ass, or a nicely filled crotch, and as often as possible. Once, while up in the truck, and rather hidden behind the tall bookcase that Jerry had turned sideways to create a small sight barrier, Tom's hand activities had managed to arouse Jerry's physical manly extremity, to the point that he had to stay in the truck and act as if he had some moving of boxes to do, until 'things' returned a little more back to normal.

Tom looked at 'it' and then at Jerry and softly stated, "Shit man. For a married guy, you sure do get all hot and horny when I reach out and touch you. I swear, I thought us gay guys got horny fast, but compared to you, we're slow. Don't you get sex a lot more often than us guys?"

"Yeah Tom, yeah we do, but fucking around with some hot hunk like you is so much more fun than the ole straight stuff, that whenever we do get a chance – like I've got today – everything is just so much more exciting. Women are women, but man – now there is a different thing. Rough, tough, solid, meaty, muscled, and usually horny as hell – that is what a real man wants to play with. Fucking a man, you can get as rough as you both want, but with a woman, you gotta keep it nice and calm, and us men, we want the rough and tumble side of sex. Us married guys keep our eyes open for something fun like you every day, and some days it works out for us, and some days it doesn't. When I saw you looking over at me while I was in the truck, I just had to pray that maybe today was gonna be one of the good days, and it sure has turned out that way. Fact is, since we really don't live that far from each other, if you're interested, I'd sure like to kinda make you my main man and use you, and let you use me, as often as either one of us needs some action. Agreed? Interested in getting something like that set up?"

"Oh my God man, you think you need to ask? Oh God Jerry, I can't believe you are actually asking me that? Hell yes I would love to set something like that up with you. You are so fucking hot that I can't believe that you are actually that interested in me, but shit man, I sure as the hell am going to take advantage of it since you're asking. Oh Jerry, I cannot believe this! I can't."

"Well, believe it man, believe it! Fact is, if we get something like this kinda set up, I've got some other daddies and hubbies that you just might like to meet, too. Us ole married guys just don't have the hideout spots that we'd like to have so that we can get it on together a little more often, so if it works out for you and me, then maybe I can bring some of my horny ole buddies around, let you meet them, and then let them do you some of the time too. Hey, gotta admit, us ole married guys just are not getting it often enough from some hot stud like you, and with you in the picture, you'll be getting some good hot sex a lot more often, and us guys will be able to get it more often too. Whenever you're available, and one of us gives you a call, it means some good ole butt fucking for you, or maybe you doing some good ole butt fucking on one of my horny buddies. Come to think of it, as often as I've thought about it, and thought it would be fun, I've never had a true group session with two or more other guys, and with you in the picture, and you having your own place, hey, maybe, just maybe, that could happen sometime. What do you think?"

"What do I think? I think great! Hey, since we'll be able to do some pre-planning, maybe we can get five or six guys together. Who are the other guys that you know and play with? Tell me about some of 'em. They're all hot guys, I'm sure – right? I mean, if you're playing with them, then I know they gotta be hot, or why would you be using 'em? You could pick out any guy that even kinda looks at you. Fact is – you ever played with some straight guy, that now plays with you all the time?"

"Oh yeah, ole Joey. Yeah, Joey and I have now been doing each other for about four or five years now. As far as I know, he's the only one that plays all the time now, but never did before he and I got together."

"Got together? How? What happened?"

"Well, I guess it was five years go now, so Joey's gotta be forty-five, now. I remember he was forty when we met, and I was twenty-three. I was driving through Georgia, on my way back from driving a truckload of stuff down to Florida, for some old couple that was moving down there. Anyway, I pulled into a filling station to fill up on gas, and this guy, Joey, came up to me and told me he saw the Illinois plates on the truck and asked if I was headed up for Illinois. I told him that yeah, I was. Then he asked if he could ride with me. His car broke down, and once he found out how much it was gonna cost to get it fixed, he just made a deal with the mechanic to just sell it to him for about two hundred bucks and not get it repaired. He was planning on taking the bus home, but then, that's when he saw the Illinois plates and thought maybe he could catch a ride with me instead. So anyway, I agreed. I figured he looked like a pretty good type of a guy, and he'd give me someone to talk to for the next couple of days."

———————

"Oh yeah, that hunk of junk! I know damn well I should not have taken a chance driving that damn thing down here and back. I wanted to come down for my daughter's college graduation in Atlanta, and I was just dumb enough to – 'just know it'd make it down and back.' But, did not! When the mechanic told me it was the transmission and what it was gonna cost to replace it, plus the expenses of staying here till he got it fixed, I just decided that the time had finally come for it to go one direction, and me another. I'm a salesman on the road for a paint company, and I usually have a company car to use, so that's why my own personal cars are never too hot, nor too new. I'll get me something when I get back to Chicago. I sure do appreciate the ride. Using the damn bus was not something that I was looking forward to."

"So Joe. Tell me about yourself. Came down to Atlanta to be at your daughter's graduation – but all by yourself? You married? I see a wedding ring. Got a wife? She didn't come?"

"Oh this wedding ring. I'm re-married. My wife now is Mary-Jane, and Diane's mother, my ex-wife is Suzanne. We divorced about ten years ago, and that was when I moved up to Chicago, and Suzanne and Diane stayed in Atlanta. Mary-Jane was not interested in going to Atlanta with me, knowing that Suzanne would be around too. And I think it did work out better that way. And especially since the ole car did its thing. So enough about me, tell me about you Jerry."

"Married – wife is Julie – we got one little girl, and expecting another – but don't know if it's another little girl or a boy. We'll find out in about six months. I work as a truck driver for a delivery company, but just local deliveries, but that's how I found out about Mr. and Mrs. Brookings that needed someone to drive their stuff down to Florida. They came into our company thinking that we did long distance moves, but I had to tell them that we did not, and the conversation went from there. They asked me if I would be interested in driving down and back if they rented a truck and of course paid all of the expenses. I had a week of vacation coming up in about a month anyway, and decided that we could use the extra cash instead of just goofing off the vacation time. They told me that they would rather hire me, since they had met me face to face, they knew where I worked and some small stuff that made them feel much better than just hiring some company they knew nothing about, nor some man that they knew nothing about either. They said they kinda liked my looks, I looked honest, and they did not want to find out sometime in the future that their truck load of stuff just happened to disappear 'somewhere' between Chicago and Tampa Bay."

"Well Jerry, if I might be so blunt as to say so, I sure as hell do agree on their statement of how they liked your looks. I know it's one man to another man, and maybe inappropriate, but I will tell you that I totally agree with them. You are one very good looking man. I sure as hell do not know how you managed to get a body like that, but Jerry, hope I'm not too far off base in just telling you, that you are one very good looking man."

"Hey Joe, never be embarrassed to tell some guy that has spent hundreds and hundreds of hours in the weight room that he looks good. That is the reason that we do it, and it's times like this, that is the payoff for all the sweat and tears we spent trying to look good."

"Well Jerry my man, you sure are one of them that looks good. I have to assume then that you started lifting weights quite early?"

"Yeah, I started while I was in the seventh grade. I was a tall skinny guy that got called 'toothpick' one day, by one of the better looking girls in the class, and I guess that was enough to piss me off, and the very next day, I was in the weight room pushing the ole iron stuff. Went from about five foot ten and a hundred and twenty-five pounds, to six foot one, and two hundred and twenty pounds before graduation day from high school. Made me a different person. During our last day of classes, we were all sitting around talking about our school days and what things we had learned or things that had really made a big impression on us. Things that made us look at life differently. I came from a small school and the class was small enough to where we could do this type of stuff, like have classroom conversations. So anyway, when it got to me – telling what had made a difference for me – I told them it as Shirley's comment back in the seventh grade when she called me a toothpick. Everybody in the room was shocked. Everybody either let out with a shocked expression, or something like, 'What? Shirley did what?!' Nobody had ever known that her comment is what changed me."

"Jerry, what did the guys say? How did they react to that?"

"Shocked too, I guess. During that time, people did make some remarks about my getting bigger, but nobody had ever really directly said anything about it. I guess they thought it was just a family thing, being black you know. There are some pretty damn hot looking black boxers, black football players and yeah, a lot of hot black construction workers, so I guess they just thought I was part of that litter. But that day did kind of change things for a me a little."

"Change things? Like what Jerry, what?"

"Well, for one thing, I found out how some of the guys looked at me, in a much more secret way. They never wanted to talk about my body before that, but once that happened, some of the private conversations changed. Of course we were out of school by then, and the restraint of being in school no longer existed, so maybe some of the guys just felt a little more free and open to express some of their feelings."

"Like what feelings, Jerry, what are you talking about?"

"Oh Joe, you know how guys love to talk about sex, but it's always gotta be about sex with girls. Well, I guess now a couple of them starting feeling a little more comfortable about talking about who they really were, and I guess maybe they thought maybe they had finally found a man that would except them for who they were, and not criticize them if they admitted that they were gay."

"Gay!? Did they think you were gay just because you worked so hard building yourself up?"

"A couple of them did, and one guy admitted that if I was not, then he wanted to convert me. And I will admit, he was a pretty damn well build guy too. He was the high school wrestling champ two years in a row. I wasn't into doing guys yet then, so he and I never got together."

"Hey wait Jerry! You just said, 'wasn't into doing guys yet then.' Am I hearing you say that you do stuff with guys now? Or anyway, did after then?"

Grinning widely and looking over toward Joe, Jerry answered. "Joe, after watching you unconsciously moving that rod of yours around back and forth just about the whole time that we've been talking about me getting myself built up, I decided it was time to admit it, that yes I do, and you ought to know right now, that if you know it or not, you are one hell of a hot man yourself. With you moving that thing back and forth, and I assume getting it comfortable someplace, I might have to assume that maybe you do too, or have, or never have, but are wishing that you had. Which is it Joe, which? Have, do you, have you in the past, or have you just thought about it and are wishing you had sometime? Which is it?"

"Oh shit man! Jerry, you got me into a conversation like I've never had before. Seriously man, have I been messing with my crotch? I didn't know it if I have been."

"Hell yes you have man, hell yes. I will admit that once I noticed it, I decide to just keep up the conversation about me and building up my ole body, just to see what reaction you'd have. So Joe, have you in the past – do you now – or, do you wish you had at some time – and if you never have – are you wanting to with me? Hey, I might be married and am a daddy, but I'm not so dumb as to pass up some good hot man sex, whenever it's available and possible. We sure are not going to make it to Chicago today, which means there is gonna be a motel room up ahead someplace for us, and I'm not gonna hide the fact that I want you in bed with me tonight, and hey, if you don't want to do that, then I guess you'll just need to find another ride the rest of the way. Hey, I'm not putting any pressure on you and what you do or do not want to do, but I've been around enough guys in my life to be able to know which ones do want to, and which ones do not want to. And I can see right now, since I mentioned your crotch and how much activity you have been giving it during this conversation, you are one of them that wants to, right?"

"Oh for God sake Jerry. Look at you! If ever there was a guy that even thought that maybe he would have sex with another guy, hell yes you would be the guy to do it with. For someone like you, someone that even looks like you, to even suggest that maybe you wanted me in bed with you, how in the hell could a man that could maybe say yes, try to say no? Jerry, I'm really getting all confused here. You are one hot God of a man, something that I'm sure any man or woman would love to lie in bed with, but Jerry, I've never been in bed with a guy, nor have I ever thought about doing it, nor even pondered if I even wanted to or not. What in the hell am I supposed to say?"

"Yes or no."

"What do you mean, 'Yes or no?' Yes or no to what?"

"Yes, you want to go to bed with me, or no, you do not. That simple. It's that simple. You do, or you do not."

Looking over toward his right slightly, and then reaching over with his right hand, Jerry very slightly placed his hand on Joe's left leg, and with no negative reaction from Joe, he slid it on down and placed it on one major hard-on. "I think I'm getting my answer – aren't I Joe?"

"Oh Jerry, you have got me so fucking confused here man. You have."

Looking over at Joe, and looking Joe in the eye, Jerry stated, "No confusion here man, none. First of all, if you did not want to do it, you would be very quick to say, 'No,' and in a very big way. But, you are not saying 'No,' and this stick I now have my hand on is definitely saying, 'Yes.' You are not the first man to have sex with a man, and without any reason to even discuss it, I know you have thought about doing it more than once, and probably many times. You are safe, you are with a friend, and finally tonight you are going to get to do something that you have wanted to do, but never thought the time would come. Well, things do change, and tonight, you are going to get the chance to do it. Nobody else will ever know. I've got a family, you've got a family, but this is just between you and me. Got it?"

"Oh Jerry, yeah I will admit that I want to be in bed with you, but I'm not sure I would just say that to any guy. Let's be honest about it Jerry. For you, or someone that looks like you, that is gonna make any person say 'Yes,' without even thinking about it. Jerry, you gotta understand that the way you are built and all the muscles on you, is gonna make any person say yes. I'm saying yes, but I'm still gonna wonder if I'm really doing the right thing or not. Right now I think it's just because of who I'm getting the chance to do it with. I mean let's face it man, having somebody like you making that kind of an offer and suggestion is gonna make about anybody do something that they never even thought about doing."

"Joe, I hear you, but I really don't agree with you. I was in Jr. college for two years, and I was on the wrestling team during those two years, and yes, there are a number of wrestlers that want another match with his competitor somewhere else, later that night – like in bed – but there are those that have no interest in some other man's body at all. And I can be one to tell you, I know, because I've actually asked a couple of those guys to come on up to my room with me, and I got some very strong negative comments. My body is not the only reason for guys to have sex with me. It is their own desire. Joe, I've known from almost the time you got in the truck, with me, that you've been hoping that I'd suggest something – someway – somehow – for us to get it going together. I saw you really checking out my crotch when we first started talking. You were looking at it like you'd never seen a crotch before. You were checking it out, big time, before you even got in the truck. I thought then, that maybe my crotch was really more important to you than getting a ride to Chicago. So now we're talking about it, and now it's out on the table that once we stop for the night, we are gonna have a good night, just enjoying each other, and letting you finally find out what sleeping in bed with a guy is like, and then of course, maybe some other actions besides just sleeping."

"Oh Jerry, I guess I'm saying "Yes," but man, I'm forty years old and I've never even touched some other guy that way. Yeah Jerry, I guess I want to or I'd be screaming to make you let me get out of this truck, but man, it's just something I've never done before."

"Joe, of course you've never done it before, I understand that, but just because you've never done it before is no reason to not do it now. Hey, maybe you've just never had a good opportunity before, but today it's there. You ever been in a situation where maybe it could have happened, if something had just been a little different? Sometime in the past, that when you kinda look back at it, maybe you just wish that things could have been a little different?"

"Oh yeah, I guess. Yeah maybe that one day a hell of a long time ago could have been one of those days."

"So, tell me. We've got about two more hours till we hit Nashville and find a good comfortable motel to use, so tell me about that day that you're thinking about. What happened?"

"Oh God man, I feel like I'm spilling all my guts to you man. I've never had a conversation like this in my entire life. Hell man, the way I grew up, if I had even thought these kinds of things, I know I would have gone to hell in a breadbasket. I just hope Mom and Dad are not up there watching down on me today from Heaven. If they are, I know damn well they'd be dying all over again."

"Uh, Joe, what happened. Your Mom and Dad are not gonna be listening, but I am. What happened?"

"I was in college, at Georgia State. I was like twenty-one years old. I had my own efficiency apartment downtown, close to campus, and one night a bunch of us were all out drinking, and I guess drinking a little too much. Well anyway, two of the dorm guys did not want to go back to campus drunk, so we decided that the three of us would all go to my place and sleep it off, and the dorm guys could sneak back in, the next morning. Well anyway, small apartment and only one bed. Yeah, we were drunk and so we all wanted to be the one that got to use the bed, and thankfully it was a double, nothing like a queen double, but more of a skinny bed, and so we all piled in. I ended up being in the middle. One guy was on the bigger side – like not skinny at all. The other guy, the one that grabbed my dick in the middle of the night, now he was pretty well built. Anyway, I'm lying there, with my briefs on, kind of asleep, but having trouble sleeping since I could not move, and anyway, he grabbed on my dick and kinda started to jerk it back and forth. He was snoring. Well, he was making it sound like he was snoring. I still think he was awake. Anyway, I moved his hand off of my dick, and then laid my own hand on my dick to kind of hide it from him. I laid there awake the rest of the night. I felt him touch me a couple of more times, and I still don't think he was asleep. Yeah, I gotta admit, that ever since that night, I've wondered if I would have acted differently, or maybe he would have been more aggressive if Danny, the kinda fat guy had not been in bed with us. I've gone to sleep many nights since then wondering if I had done things right, or if I should have just let him jerk on me and then let things develop in a different way. His grabbing my dick, and the other couple of times that I felt his hand touching me someplace kinda private was never mentioned nor talked about. I still think he wanted me to think he was asleep, but I never have. I know for damn sure he was wanting some action with me, and I still wonder what and how I would have handled it if Danny had not been there. Maybe I should have just gone ahead and slipped my briefs off, and let him play."

"Oh, so for maybe about twenty years now, you've had that night in the back of your mind, and have kinda been pissed at yourself for not letting something happen – right?"

"Yeah Jerry, yeah. Yes, I gotta admit that night has been in the back of my mind ever since. So, I guess maybe that's why I'm telling you that, 'Yes,' I'll go through with this tonight just so I can finally find out if I goofed up that night, or did I do the right thing. I gotta be honest with you though, cause I don't want you being mad at me if things just don't work out for me tonight. I'm gonna do it, but Jerry, I'm afraid that once we start, I may not be able to follow through and I might have to call it all off. You understand?"

"Oh yes man, oh yes. You still gotta remember you are not the first man to have man-to-man sex. From what you've already told me, I know that during your entire childhood you were pretty well controlled about what you could or could not do, and what you were supposed to think and what you were not supposed to think – right?"

"Oh yeah, you're right. I kinda think that is why it did not work out for Suzanne and I. Just too damn much parent involvement. We could not make a move without a whole bunch of criticism from my parents. Fact is, that's the reason I moved up to cold old Chicago after we got divorced. The time had come for me to go live my own life, and not theirs."

"So what I think I'm hearing here is, that one night while in college is not the only time that maybe you could have had some good ole man-to-man sex, but the locks on you were just so tight, that you knew that if you did ever let some guy play with that dick of yours, that your whole life would come apart – right?"

"Well, I never thought about it that way, but, 'Yes!' Yeah, even after I left the Atlanta area, I was still afraid to maybe let something happen, with someone. Yeah, there were times right after I moved to Chicago that I kinda wanted to go see if maybe something – whatever – could happen, but I was just so damned afraid that if I did something with someone, that somehow the words would get back to Atlanta, and Mom and Dad. You know man, once I've had the opportunity to really talk about my life like I am today, and with someone like you, I'm really starting to see myself a whole lot better. Yeah Jerry, I'm ready. I'm real ready, and now I'm gonna finally be honest with myself and admit I'm anxious."

"Good, I'm glad to hear that. Took a long time to finally really see yourself, but I kinda think maybe you finally have."

"Yeah Jerry, but I still gotta wonder if I'd be so quick to say yes if it was to some other guy that was a little more normal, and not looking like one of the bronze statues that they have all over Europe. Seriously man, you are one fucking hot looking human being. You know something Jerry? Now that I kinda understand myself a little better than I did a little earlier today, I did not know it, but I now kinda think that the real reason I approached you back there at the gas station, was not so much about not wanting to use the bus, but rather my unaware desire to be with you, and get to know you. Yeah, like you told me earlier, I guess maybe I was handling my crotch a lot more than I realized, and that was because the real me was anxious to get to see you naked, and the mental part of me was still saying, 'No, no!' Okay, now that I'm all frustrated and anxious, can I pull my dick out and let you see it? Nobody will see it up here in the truck will they?"

"Hey, go right ahead man, go right ahead. I was just about ready to ask you to do that, but decided to wait and see if you'd suggest it, and you did. Pull that baby out. Let me see it. I saw a road sign back there that the next roadside rest is coming up, so I'm gonna pull off in there and we're gonna see if there is anybody in the men's room, and if not, I'm gonna see what the tip of it tastes like for a quick minute. Okay?"

As Joe did open his fly and pulled down his briefs, he did manage to pull out his hard-on, and Jerry let out with a very complementary, "Oh, wow man! Hey, that is nice! I'm getting real anxious for us to get to a motel, so I can take that whole thing all the way down in me. You just might find yourself doing some butt fucking tonight with that big thing too. Damn man, when I reached over there and put my hand on it, it sure did not feel like that much meat in there. And Joe, you've never had some guy suck on that, not even in a restroom?"

"Nope, no, never. I know I've seen some guys looking at it when I was taking a piss, and there have been a number of times that I just know, that if I had kinda offered it to them, they would have taken it, but you know me and my sick mental hang-ups. I just always tucked it back in my pants and then wondered later what could have happened, if I had turned toward them and kind of flipped it up and down. Damn, now I wish I had."

Only a couple more miles down the road, and the roadside rest area appeared, and Jerry said, "Hey Joe. Here comes the roadside rest area, tuck that big boner back in there and let's go see if we've got ourselves an empty restroom that we can use."

Jerry pulled the truck into the truck parking area, and told Joe, "I know the truck area is really for the big trucks, but I always use 'em, cause that's where the hot interesting drivers are. I always use the restroom closest to the truck parking, cause once in a while you might just happen to go in, right at the right time. There's quite a few trucks parked in here right now, so let's hope that maybe we might just happen in the door at the right time, as some good ole trucker man is getting a load dumped down in his throat. That is the real right time to just happen in, when a man is right in the middle of shooting off, and he can't get it done in time to hide his rod, and the other guy is squatting there with cum dripping out of his mouth."

"Jerry – Jerry! Do guys really do that in the restrooms? Do they do that? I mean, yeah I've always heard about restroom activities, but I just always thought that was wild talk. Do guys really suck each other off in restrooms out along the highway?"

"Hey, there's probably more sex going on in highway restrooms than in most houses within five miles of 'em."

As Jerry and Joe entered the restroom, two men made some actions of rather quickly getting apart, and the shorter bald man just simply walked out the door, leaving his restroom friend standing there with his boner sticking out of his uniform pants. A work uniform – not police nor military uniform – but none the less, a very promising sight. Looked like maybe a city or county employee, that type of a uniform, and obviously a man that does not do his work behind a desk. There was no wonder the bald man was going after it. He was hanging out a very significant dick, thick and strong – just like the massive arms he had hanging to his sides.

Jerry looked at the man, a man about thirty three or thirty four years old, looked down at the dick the man was now trying to quickly get hidden, and he said, "Hey, don't bother. Don't hide it, let's see it. Looks damp. Guess maybe we interrupted something going on in here, didn't we?" Then bending over with his mouth directly in front of the boner, Jerry pulled it back out from being partly replaced back into the neat uniform pants and said, "Let me taste it. Looks tasty. Does it need to be finished off?"

Joe stood there with his mouth hanging wide open at the sight, as Jerry quickly sucked the eight inches of stiff dick into his mouth and gave it a couple of very quick, solid, and firm sucks. Pulling off of it, he then looked up at the owner of his sucking stick, and asked, "Hey, where you headed for? Headed up for the Chicago area?"

The man acting very puzzled about the questions softly replied, "Yeah, kinda that direction. Not all the way to Chicago, but up that way, why?"

"Cause my buddy and I are headed up that way too, and we're going to be spending the night in Nashville someplace, and I was just wondering if you might maybe would like to come visit us at our motel and really get that big boner sucked off good for a change."

As the man stood there with his dick still out on display, he replied, "Yeah, maybe."

Jerry looked at him with a quizzed expression on his face and asked, "Maybe? What's the maybe? Maybe, due to what?"

"Due to if I get to see your dick now or not. I wanna see what you're offering and hanging down there, then I'll let you know."

And with that rather straightforward request, or instruction if that is what it was intended to be – and Jerry took it to be an instruction – he immediately opened his Levi's, pulled them down, allowing both men to now see that he wore no underwear, and let it all fall out. Both men, the man with the exposed dick still sticking out, and Joe, both let out with an enthusiastic, "Oh man!"

The 'extra man,' whose name was Bill, as they later found out, looked at Jerry's dick, then looked over at Joe and asked, "What surprised you so? Haven't you ever seen your buddy's dick?"

Rather quickly, Jerry explained to Bill what the situation was, and how Joe has never had any man-to-man experiences, and tonight was going to be his virgin entry into that activity.

Looking at Bill, Jerry then asked, "So, what's your decision? Interested or not? You've seen my dick, and if you meet up with us, you'll see it a lot more, stuck in both ends if you want, and you can help me teach Joe here some of the finer things of life. What do you say?"

"If you're telling me that you're gonna fuck my ass with that bat and stick it down my throat, I'm on – I'm definitely on. Shit yes, wow! I've never had that much pushed up in my ass before, and I sure as hell have never tried to swallow that much steak all at once before, so yeah man, count me in – count me in. But how am I gonna know where you're at?"

"Couple of days ago I made the drive south, and stayed in a motel in Nashville and did not know I'd be staying there again, but I've got their name and address on a piece of stationary paper in my truck, so we'll just plan on going back there, so we'll know how to find each other."

"Hey, I don't have any kind of a room reservation made anyplace, so I'll just plan on staying at the same motel. That'll make it easier, right?"

"Yeah, right! Good idea. So tell you what. Give me and Joe here a minute to take a pee, which I really gotta do, and then as long as nobody comes walking in the door, I told him I wanted to pull his dick out and get a quick taste of it, and then we'll head on out and get that address for you. Okay?"

"Hey sounds like a plan man, sounds good. I plan on getting something to eat once I get to Nashville, so you guys wanna find something to eat with me?"

Joe and Jerry both replied with a "Yeah. Let's do that."

Of course Jerry already had his dick out and ready, and as he approached a urinal, he immediately started shooting some warm yellow water into the urinal, and Joe followed suit as he too got it all pulled out and aimed. Jerry of course looked over and took a good eyeful of the rod of meat that he just knew he was going to be sucking on in just a moment or two – well – as long as nobody else came into the restroom.

As the two men took their peeing action, Bill stood close by admiring both dicks. Joe finished first, quickly followed by Jerry. Rather quickly, Jerry turned Joe toward him, quickly stooped down, grabbed onto Joe's stick, put it in his mouth and sucked. Three good sucks and he then pulled off, looked up at Bill and asked, "Want to be man number two on this dick? Nobody's ever had it in his mouth until right now, so if you want to see what a good virgin dick can feel like in your mouth, here it is." Then looking up at Joe, Jerry did ask, "Okay with you Joe? Should have asked you, but is it okay if he tries it out too?"

Almost breathlessly Joe tried to reply with an, "Oh yeah, oh yeah! Oh yeah please do, yeah do it."

Bill immediately stooped down, grabbed Joe's rod and sucked it to the bottom of his throat. As Jerry stood back up, he said, "Hey do it quickly. I wanna get out of here before somebody else comes in."

With three strong sucks, Bill pulled off and simply said, "God men, let's get to that motel! I've got me some meat to take care of tonight. This trip is turning out to be one hell of a lot more fun than I expected it to be."

With everybody re-arranging themselves, and getting all prim and proper, they went out to Jerry's truck and got out the motel stationary, so that they could give Bill the information. In addition to the motel information, the three men did conduct a rather formal introduction as to just who each man was, like sharing names. They agreed that whoever got to the motel first, was to check in, then the following truck would ask if the other man had arrived yet, and if so, get a room next door if possible. Bill suggested that if they got to the motel first, do ask if they had any rooms that shared a common door between the two rooms. That suggestion set very well with Jerry and Joe. "Good idea," both men responded.

With information in hand, Bill turned, pointed at his truck and said, "That's my truck, the red Ram. I'm sure we'll probably be seeing each other on the road on into Nashville, but if not, I'll see you at the motel."

———————————

"So, from that day forward, ole Joe, or as I now call him, Joey, and I have hit it with each other about every other week when he's down in this part of the state. He still sells paint, but for a different company now, and his schedule gets him down here every two weeks. He stays in the same place, each visit, so he just calls me and tells me when he's gonna be here, and we do our thing for part of a night."

"But hey, that first night, that night with that Bill guy, how did that work out?"

"Oh that worked out perfectly. Joe learned a lot that night, and that Bill, he is one hell of a playmate. Joe got sucked off that night and did a little bit of butt playing with both Bill and me, and he had a chance to kinda get over his old childhood mental restrictions as to what he should do, and what he should not do, but I will be honest with you and tell you that most of the good activity that night was between Bill and I. I kinda think maybe things worked out better that way. Joe saw some good ole hard-core man-to-man sex, but he was not forced into doing stuff that he felt uncomfortable with. Over the years he's now gotten into those types of activities, but for that night, it was a good learning session for him."

"Do you and that Bill ever see each other anymore?"

"No, no. Wish we did, but that was a one night stand between him and me."

"So what did you two do that night that Joe just watched? What happened?"

"Oh, that Bill guy was a real player. Hell, he taught me some stuff that night too."

"Like what? What'd he teach you?"

"Well, I think the most important thing he taught me was, that getting an ass rimming, feels damn good! I'd never had my ass licked on and chewed on, like I got that night from him, and now I never turn it down. And I'd never had most of a man's hand up in my ass before that night, but I sure did that night. And, I found out that night why some guys like to get fisted. Since Joe watched that action, that night, he brought it up later – like, oh maybe a year later – and told me he wanted to try that, so now I get a fist up in my ass, once or twice a month, whenever old Joey feels like doing it."

"Well, does he ask you if you want it, or does he just do it without asking?"

"I know it's gonna sound kinda of selfish, but the way we play, we never ask the other guy if he wants something or not, we just do it. Both ways. I guess we've just moved into a relationship that each of us just takes control, and the other person is happy with that. So, in other words, when we do get together, we never know what is gonna happen, nor who is going to be the boss. We just get into something, and let everything develop from that point."

"Julie doesn't know about Joey, does she?"

"Oh hell no! No. She doesn't have any idea that I play with guys, so be real careful when she's around, okay?"

"Oh yeah I will. I don't want to do anything wrong, believe me."

"Thanks. Well, I think maybe we've goofed off enough time getting this truck unloaded. Let's get the rest of this stuff out of here, and if Julie is not back by that time, I'll give her a call and tell her I'm taking the truck back. Then if you're in the mood, so to say, maybe we can stop by your place for a minute or two. Okay?"

"Hell yes that is okay! I want to! Especially now that I know you like getting your ass rimmed and chewed on. I am, gonna get to do that, right?"

"Hell yes, if you want to. Come on, let's get this stuff in the house. If you're wanting to kiss my ass and chew on it some, I'm getting real anxious. Hell, I thought today was gonna be a real bummer getting nothing else, but moved, but I like the way it's turning out. The way you're talking now, is getting me really anxious to get something like that going."

After about another hour of 'getting stuff off of the truck,' they finally had the truck emptied, and had managed to get each other's crotch grabbed, numerous times. The truck was emptied, and Julie had not yet returned. Jerry said, "I'm gonna call Julie and see just what's going on over there, and tell her that I'm gonna take the truck back, and get some cash out of the ATM so I can pay you."

After a brief conversation, Jerry hung-up, and turned toward Tom. "Well, I guess maybe our planning has changed. Julie just told me that the kids are gonna stay over at Grandma's for the night, and Julie told me to come over there after I take the truck back. We're having dinner over there, I guess. So maybe that is working out good for us. I didn't tell her that the truck was now empty, and that we were gonna head out for the rental place. Let's get this place shut up and get on the road. It's been almost two weeks since ole Joey's been in town, so it's been that long since I've had a chance to taste some good ole white cock cum, and now I'm getting real anxious for yours, and I'm wanting to see just how your tongue feels stuck up in my little ole tree hole, back there. The last thing I've had up in there was Joey's fist when he was here in town, so I'm anxious to get it played with again."

Chapter Three: Where's The Bedroom Man?

"Well this is my 'abode," Tom told Jerry as they entered his apartment after turning in the rental truck, and also stopping by an ATM to get the money Jerry owed Tom for his help unloading the truck.

As Jerry handed the fifty bucks to Tom, he said, "Here guy. Here is what I owe you for the help today, but let me tell you – I really do think I'm the one that's getting paid, since, our moving, and our little looking at each other through the truck mirror, has let me know you, and you know me. Come here baby, I wanna give you one hell of a hug and feel that tight ass of yours, and feel it and grab it like really good, and really strong."

Tom moved over closer to Jerry, reached around Jerry's waist, leaned into Jerry and felt the two very strong hands, get reached around him and each hand, grab one solid hunk of butt muscle. Jerry squeezed and tugged at Tom's butt.

"Oh yeah man, oh yeah!" Tom expressed as he felt the strength of Jerry's hands grabbing and squeezing his ass.

"Oh Jerry, I've wanted this ever since I saw you in the truck mirror, and then of course at the restaurant. I still can't believe I had the guts to go into that restaurant, once I realized, that is where you were headed. I could have gotten my ass in some really big trouble if maybe you were really thinking I was some kind of a goofy nut. And besides, I never even wondered if there was possibly somebody else in the truck, besides you, that I couldn't see. Damn, things could have gone really bad if you were different than I was hoping."

"Well, let me tell you guy, I am just damn glad you were available and willing to help me unload today, cause when I came over to your table to ask you 'if you knew anybody,' I would have been in real shit if you were not available and willing, cause then to try and cover things from Julie, and not tell her what I was really up to, I would have had to try and find someone else to help me. And I am damn sure, if I had found someone else, his ass sure would not have been this tight and solid, even if he would have let me grab it. Oh thank goodness everything worked out okay – and like we both wanted."

"Yeah Jerry – so far so good though."

"What? What? What'd you mean by that?"

"What I mean by that is – I still have not gotten you all stripped down and good and naked, and my mouth on that tanker of a dick that I've been anxious for all day. Before we found each other today, I was here reading some hot gay stories on the computer, and of course I like to read the stories about the little white guy that gets it on with a big, bold, black, beautiful hunk like you, and swallows his cock down his throat and also takes it up in his ass, and now I feel like I'm in the story. I'm the little white guy, and you are the big, bold, black, beautiful, hunk that is gonna give it to me in both ends – right?"

As Jerry hugged and grabbed onto Tom's tight-bubbled butt even tighter, he replied. "Oh, so you think you're the little white guy that gets it from the big black guy, right?"

"Yeah, yeah! That is what I'm planning on!"

"Well, just what in the hell are we gonna do then, if the big black guy wants to get some from the little white guy? Then what?"

"Then we do it! Hell yes, then we do it! Mine sure ain't as big as yours, but I sure am willing to give you all I've got. I just gotta admit though, that when reading those hot stories – to me – it's always when the big black man has got his big thick stiff rod stuck up in the white guy, that really turns me on. Hell, just reading that stuff, I get a boner on me and it only takes one small touch of my dick to make it shoot off like a cannon. And, yeah, when you finally get that rod of yours up in my ass, I know damn well, I will be shooting off like a whole brigade of cannons."

"Well, damn it then, let's do it!" Jerry rather quickly said, as he let loose of Tom's butt and then asked, "Where's the bedroom man, where's it at?"

Quickly Tom and Jerry headed down the hall toward the bedroom, and as they entered, Tom immediately stripped everything off as quickly as he could, and Jerry followed suit.

Tom grabbed some lube off of a bed stand, handed it to Jerry and said, "I know I took that log up in my ass over at your house, but here, use some of this, cause I want that damn thing up in me a hell of a lot longer and deeper than I got it earlier, so lube your rod good, cause I really want it."

"You want it up in you deeper than you got it earlier? Is that what you just said? How in the hell can I put it up in you any deeper than I did earlier since I had the whole fucking thing up in you then? Tom, my man, you had the whole thing!"

Turning his head as far as possible to try and answer Jerry, Tom said, "I know, I know. But man, this time you're gonna be on my back and lying on me and my butt, and I want you to really push good and hard so it'll go in, deeper and deeper. Oh man, I want all of you up in there. Seriously man, if you can put more than just your dick up in there, do it! I want you in me!"

As Jerry prepared his rod for entry, he aimed it at the hole, and then asked, "Uh Tom. You just said you want more of me than just my dick up in there. Is that right? Is that what you said?"

"Yeah, yeah I did. Why?"

"Cause from the way you are begging for more, I'm starting to wonder if maybe you are actually telling me that you want me to do some fisting back here, right?"

"Oh shit – oh man, I don't know. Yeah, yeah I think! Jerry I think I do but I'm afraid to admit it. I guess when I was saying that, yeah maybe that is what I was trying to say, without actually saying it. You told me earlier about you getting fisted by your buddy, Joey, and yes I do admit, just the mental idea of you being the man to do it with, makes me want to do it. I've never been fisted before, and I will admit I kinda think the reason it sounds kinda exciting to me this time, is totally because of you. Seriously, if some other guy had mentioned it or told me he wanted to do it, I'm not so sure I'd even say I would think about it, but with you, I guess maybe I'm willing to let you be in total control to do whatever you want, and however you want. Jerry I've never been with a man as hot as you, and I admit, if you tell me to go jump off of the bridge, I'd probably go and do it."

"Good, cause right now, you lie there! I'm gonna pound you and this little hot white ass as good and as strongly as I can, and I'm gonna make sure you know that right now, you have got one hot, and horny, big, black man, with his big, black, thick, stiff, rod, up in your butt and he is gonna use it for all it's worth. Lie still man, you are about to get the fucking of your life and I am gonna make sure this is one fucking that you will never forget!"

And for the next ten or fifteen minutes, Tom did get the fucking of his life, and Jerry GAVE Tom the fucking of his life. Jerry told, little white Tom, that he was in for one hell of a fucking, and he made sure he'd never forgot what was happening during the entire time.

"Lie still man, lie still! I am fucking you back here, and I am gonna be fucking you good and hard! I've found me an ass that is ready for it, and I am ready to give it to you. You are getting it in the butt man, you are getting it good and strong! I'm using everything I've got on it! I haven't fucked any good tight and hard ass like this one, for a hell of a long time, and I'm liking it!"

Getting pounded good and hard and rough, Tom had troubles trying to say anything, but he did utter, "Oh yeah man, oh yeah! Fuck me man, please fuck me hard."

"Your ass is gonna be red and sore when I get done back here, hang on man, I'm just getting started on it man – I'm just getting started!"

"Oh good, oh yeah do me man, do me!" Tom did manage to get out.

"I'm pounding your ass like I've never pounded an ass before! Your ass is so much better than trying to pound on some woman and having sex with a little soft thing that just can't take it! With this ass I can pound it in and out, and get rough and really with it, and get to it in a big strong way! I like it, I like it!"

"Yeah, yeah, do me man, do me! Yeah harder man, do me harder!"

"You are gonna be black and blue back here when I get done! Man, you are gonna be sore, man, you are gonna have one sore ass!"

"Okay, okay I can take it man, give it to me, make me black and blue – fuck me hard!"

Pounding on Tom's ass as hard as he could manage, Jerry said, "Hey, grab that headboard man, cause you're about to pump up and down like some little rabbit out in the field. Hang on tight, cause I'm fucking the hell out of you and this cute little white ass, and I'm fucking enjoying it! I'm getting what I've never had before, and damn man, I like it! Your big black man is fucking the little white ass like you read about in your stories! And the big black man and his big black dick are having one hell of a hot and good time doing it. He likes it! Oh fucking shit man, I am about exhausted! I'm using everything I've got in me, to pound this little white ass of yours man, I am!"

"When I get done here, I'm not sure if I'm gonna have enough strength to get up and off of you – but while I'm still here – you are gonna get it like crazy man, just fucking plain crazy! Lie there man – I'm getting some ass and I'm liking what I'm getting, and I'm trying my damnest to give you everything I've got, so hang on man. I'm gonna pound you till the day falls through, or I do, one or the other!"

"Yeah, yeah man, do me, do me! Oh Jerry, fuck the hell out of me please, fuck me like you've never fucked some ass before! Hard man! Really, really hard!"

"Oh God, I hope you can feel the end of my dick coming out of your mouth. I want my dick up in you that fucking far! I want it in all the way through you! I want it sticking out of your mouth! Oh shit man, you have got one hell of a nice ass to pound on, and drive my rod into, and as far and as fast as I can! I am fucking you man! I am fucking the hell out of you!"

Tom's main accomplishment in speaking right then, was a simple, "Yeah man, yeah!"

"Tom my man, you are getting it, you are getting it. Oh man, oh yeah – oh yeah – you are about to get it, and I mean get it, cause it feels like you are gonna get a hell of a lot of it! Hey man – hang on – hang on! I'm letting loose man! I'm cumming man! I'm cummmmmmin! Oh shit man! Oh God! Oh – I have not shot off like that in years! Oh man, you okay? You okay? I just filled your ass full man, I know I did. You've got juices up in your butt like crazy man, you have gotta be full of cum. Oh man! I let it all fly! Oh man, you're gonna have my baby man, you gotta. No guy can get shot up in the ass like that and not get knocked-up! Oh Tom, I wish you could! Oh man, I wish I could get you knocked-up! Oh man, that would be proof of what this fucking was all about! I'd have me a little light skinned tan Tommy running around that I could point at and say, 'I remember that day.'"

With Jerry still pumping and pounding as hard as ever, when he started letting Tom know that he was just about to shoot off, there was absolutely no way that Tom could have even attempted any type of a reply. For the past ten minutes or more, he had totally and completely submitted his entire existence over to Jerry, and his exuberance of giving Tom the wildest and roughest fucking that Tom had ever had. And at the same time, doing the best fucking that he had ever experienced – in his mind anyway – for his entire life.

Breathing very heavily, and collapsing completely down on top of Tom and with his own near breathless body, Jerry attempted to tell Tom that he had just had the best sex and fucking that he had ever had, but the air just was not there, for talking. Both men laid still, quietly, and motionless for a few minutes before Jerry finally did roll over and off of Tom's exhausted body. Both men were totally covered with sweat. Both men were still breathing heavily and deeply, trying to regain some normal breathing capacity.

After recovering enough to at least be slightly functional, Jerry told Tom that he simply did have to get over to his mother-in-law's house, or he was gonna have way too much explaining to do. "You and I have really hit the jackpot today finding each other, and I sure don't want to screw it up now, by letting her know what's been going on. We gotta play things cool."

Tom suggested that Jerry run in and take a shower to make sure he did not have any extra male fragrances on him, and as Jerry came back from the bathroom, he asked, "You mentioned earlier this evening, that you're gonna be taking a ride down to Memphis in a couple of weeks, right?"

"Yeah, I am. I gotta take a load of equipment down for my Dad's company. Why? Why you asking?"

"Cause I've got a sister that lives down there, and I just thought maybe, that if you wanted some company, I might ride down there with you if possible, and if you want."

"Oh hell yes I do, oh hell yes! Oh Jerry can you? Hey, we'll be down there overnight, and we could stay together that night, right?"

"Well, that was my thinking. I wouldn't be staying at Sis's house anyway, and this would give me a reason for just a stop by and see her, and also at the same time, give you and me a reason to be gone, overnight. I could tell Julie that you asked if I could come along to help with the equipment and help with some of the driving."

"Oh man, what a great idea. I'm gonna be leaving here on Friday morning the 14th, and I plan on being back the next night, but if we don't rush too much – and maybe need to take things a little slower – then be back sometime Sunday." And with one very big grin on his face, he added, "But you know, that would mean that we'd have to spend an extra night – together – someplace, right?"

"Right you are man. Right! Not a problem with me, no problem at all!" Then acting as if it is a joke, Jerry then added,

"And hey, if the truck breaks sown someplace, we just might have to spend "another night" together, someplace!"

"Julie will let you go, right? She won't have a problem with letting you go, will she?"

"No that's not gonna be a problem. I have not seen Sandra for a couple of years now, and Julie has been pushing me to go down and see her, and so this planning will work out nicely. I've got a bunch of vacation days coming to me, so I'll use one of them, and I'll just tell her that for me, it's gonna be a free ride down and back, and your Dad's company is gonna pay for us to be there overnight, or – as we might find out later – the two nights."

"Tom this is gonna work out great. Now your Dad won't care if I ride along will he?"

"Oh hell no! Hell, he'll be glad cause then he won't feel like he needs to send one of the other guys down with me. No, this is gonna be great! Jerry, this is great! I was hoping when I saw you in that mirror, that I'd get to meet you, and things are just working out one hell of a lot better than I ever expected. I make these kind of trips often, and of course each one is an overnighter, and if you can go along with me on some of them, it's gonna really make it one hell of a lot more fun, and besides, we'll talk Dad into paying you for going, instead of paying one of the guys overtime, for going. Definitely a payday for me, and a little extra cash for you, which'll help Julie agree that, 'Yeah, you need to go help Tom deliver that stuff.' Man, I never thought that watching some guy in a truck mirror was gonna pay back like this one is today. I'm not gonna have to sit at home anymore and read those hot gay stories about the little white guy that gets it in the butt by some big, bold, black and beautiful muscle man. I'm gonna be that little white guy that's getting it in the butt here, as often as possible, and in some motel room along the road, as often as possible, too! Oh you do not realize how scared I was when

I followed you and your wife into that restaurant. I was afraid that you were gonna think I was some goofy guy, and now I get to be your man, for you to use me and pound me, any way you want, and hopefully as often as you want! Oh thank God for that mirror!"

Camping with David

"Come on man, come on Jason – come on! What in the hell did you think I meant when I suggested that we go up to the lake and campout for the weekend and have some fun together? What in the hell did you think I was talking about? I wasn't talking about playing cards man!"

"David – David – nothing like this! I thought you just meant coming up here and doing some camping and just hanging out for the weekend and – I don't know, maybe doing some hiking or something! But shit man, not this!"

"Hey guy! You've known all along that I've been anxious to get in your pants, haven't you? If you don't, then I'm telling you now! I mean man, I'm grabbing at you all the time, whenever I can get away with it, and face it man, every time you go take a piss, I go take a piss too, don't I? Hell, half of the time I have trouble pissing, but at least I get a chance to check out that 'big long black swinging rod,' of yours! Jason, you've got to have figured it out by now, that I've been trying to get you off someplace nice and quiet, like this place, ever since we started working together! Shit man, every other time I tried to set something up, there always ended up being somebody else there and nothing worked out for me. You knew that didn't you?"

"No, hell no I did not! Besides David, you and I both have wives back home. I don't play with guys! I'm married and have got a little boy and another kid on the way! David, you're married too, you don't play with guys, do you? Do ya!!?"

"Uhh – well yeah, when I get a chance. Jason – big strong black guys turn me on and have, ever since high school, playing football with the big strong black guys, either the ones on my team or guys on the other team. Shit man, I loved tackling 'em. When I did, I laid there on 'em, just as long as I could, and as long as I could get away with it! I think one of the guys from over on the Brookside team kinda knew I was there a little longer than necessary, once. At first he acted kind of mad, but then later I think he was wanting me to do it again. Once when I threw him down, he grabbed me kinda funny, like he didn't want me to get up off of him. I always wondered about him after that, but he was from Brookside and not Central. I never got to find out, but he was one hell of a hot looking and big, strong, built black guy, and he turns me on yet, just thinking about him! I wanted to shower with him so fucking bad!"

"But David, that was back in high school. That's been years ago! You graduated what, eight, nine years ago? You played with guys since then?"

"Yeah, but just black guys! Big black guys! Jason, I told you, black guys turn me on. I've never done anything with a white guy, but black guys – let's face it man, guys like you make me hot! Come on Jason, come on, let me suck you, just suck on you."

"David, I don't play with guys! I never have. I didn't know that was why you wanted us to come camping, really I didn't."

"Jason, I thought you knew what I wanted. Hey man, remember that day when we had to duck into that closet to let those guys with that cart of lumber get past us and when I had to lean up against you and I told you something like, 'Hey man, I like this, you feel good.' What in the hell did you think I meant? What about the time when Jimmy was talking about being out on the family farm and happened to watch the stud fucking the mare and I turned and kinda quietly told you that I wanted to be your mare?"

"David, I thought you were just trying to be funny! I thought that was some kind of a sick joke or something."

"Jason, how many times have I, kinda jokingly, grabbed onto that crotch of yours, whenever we were off by ourselves, and I managed to make some kind of a stupid joke or comment and then jokingly said something like, 'Yeah they do it like this,' and then grabbed your crotch for a second or so? Hey man, all those stupid comments or jokes were all just to give me a reason to reach out at you and get my hand on that big bulge you got there! Come on Jason, I wanna do some playing! Come on man, let me see it!"

"David, I've never done anything with a guy, seriously man, I've never done the guy thing!"

"Come on Jason, a guy built like you and hung like you are, and you're telling me that no guy has ever gotten to you? You played sports in school didn't you? Somebody – some guy, has had to have gotten to you and that dick of yours at some time or another. You used to shower with other guys didn't you? Didn't any guy in the shower ever go for that dick of yours? Come on man, you can't convince me that no guy has ever gotten to that stick of meat!"

"In our school the coach was always in the locker room until we got done showering. He always told us it was to keep us from flipping each other with the end of a wet towel. He said that's why he had to stay there until everybody was done and they had put stuff away."

"Put stuff away!? Put stuff away!!!? Jason – Jason, it was probably your dick that he was really talking about! Coaches do not hang out in the locker room waiting on guys to get dressed. Did you ever see him checking out your dick? Shit man, he was looking at dicks and asses, not worrying about guys getting flipped with some towel!"

"You think so? You really think so?"

"Hell yes man, hell yes! Hey Jason, how many guys were in your school? I mean, like how many would be in the locker room at the same time?"

"Oh, probably maybe twenty or twenty five. I don't really know."

"How many of those guys were big hung black guys?"

"Well, I don't know if they were what you'd call 'big hung,' but there were about fifteen or sixteen of us black guys, most of the time."

"Your coach! Was he a black man or a white man? Black or white?"

"Well, he was white. He was a white guy."

"Hell, I knew it man, I knew it! He's a white guy just like me that gets all hot and bothered once I'm around guys built and looking like you! He was the same. Hey, was he married?"

"No, no he was a single guy, and our school was his first job out of college."

"Is he still there? Do you know?"

"No, he got in some kind of trouble with the school board about two years ago, and he left."

"What kind of trouble, you know?"

"Well, all I know is, what Junior – my kid brother told me – and that was that someone saw him and one of the seniors in a dark bar together somewhere, and the school board told him to leave."

"You know who that senior was?"

"Yeah, Todd Weaver, a friend of Junior's"

"Is Todd a black guy?"

"Yeah, he is. Yeah, now I know what you're thinking! You know what – I never really thought about it, but yeah, Todd left town right after graduation that year too. You're telling me that Coach Davidson and Todd were doing the stuff, aren't you?"

"Hey, can't say it for sure, but I'll just about bet a million that your coach was checking you and all the other guys out like some watch dog when you were hanging it out loose, and he and that Todd guy finally got it on, and are probably living together someplace today! Hell man, that could have been either you or your brother. I'd almost kinda guess that Todd's pretty well hung. Is he? Do you know?"

"Yeah he is. He was with a group of us one day out skinny dipping, swimming in the nude, and yeah, he was pretty well the center of attention every time he got out of the water. Junior told me that he always seemed to like to show it off some, whenever he could."

"Oh! Okay then! I was probably right! He showed it off to the coach, and the coach liked it and took it! Hey man, if he was hung longer than what you've got, hell man, I don't blame the coach! Shit man, he just might have gotten himself a nice big prized piece of meat there!"

"How in the hell do you know what I've got? All you've ever seen is when I took a piss."

David, the thirty-year-old white, six foot two, two hundred and twenty five pound blond co-worker said, "Holly shit man! When you take a piss, you've got more dick sticking out there than most men have when they've got a hard-on! Come on Jason, pull it out and let me really see it, come on!"

"David – David. Come on now man, I don't show my dick to people. Come on man."

"Hey Jason, come on! It's just you and me, and besides, I've grabbed it before, course not out of your pants, but anyway, and I've watched you pull it out and piss a lot of times. Come on man, let me see it! We're out here all by ourselves, way back here in the woods, nobody else is around, and it's just you and me. Come on man, let me see it!"

"David, does your wife know you like to look at guys' dicks? I mean, look and whatever else you do? Does she know!?"

"No – let's face it, that's not something that I discuss with her. She did ask me once why I seemed to have so many black friends, and I didn't tell her the real reason, but then I reminded her that I do happen to work for a company that's owned by a black man. I'm not gonna tell her about what we do here this weekend either! None of her business – but that sure don't stop me from doing what I wanna do! Come on! Let me see it! Hey, I've been honest with you and I've been pretty straight forward in telling you just what in the hell turns my buttons on – you – so come on man, help me out here. Nobody is ever gonna know. Come on, let me undo your pants and let me take it out! Okay, okay – can I?"

Jason, the twenty-one year old, hot looking and muscle built black construction worker, simply stood there, rather confused, and really did not know just what to do. David's advances were totally unexpected, and somewhat of a shock. He admitted that yes, there had been quite a few times when he rather wondered just why David had done some of the things that he had done, or maybe said some of the things that he had said, but he never expected anything like this to happen! The idea that he was a 'turn on' to David was a pleasant thought though. Maybe the hours working out in the weight room were actually doing some good, if another guy was liking the way he looked. As he stood there completely confused, he really did not know what to do – rather than just maybe let David unzip his pants, let him pull it out, look at it, and just get it over with! Just let the guy look at it and get it done!

Both men stood face to face, and chest to chest, and David slowly reached forward and slowly unbuckled Jason's belt. Slowly he unsnapped the waistband, and slowly unzipped Jason's Levi shorts. He looked eyeball to eyeball with Jason, and realized that he was finally getting to do what he had been begging for, ever since they got camp set up. Slowly he slid his hands inside of Jason's shorts and with a slight tug, managed to let them slide down off of Jason's handsome tight muscled ass cheeks.

Slightly licking his lips and also allowing his bare chest to touch Jason's bare chest, he then slid his fingertips into the top of Jason's Fruit of the Loom briefs and then, as he stooped, he slid his face down the length of Jason's beefy construction built pecks and pulled the tight white briefs down past Jason's muscled ass and his six inch long limp black sausage. Finally David had that dick, that beautiful thick black dick, the one that he had been grabbing at (usually as a joke) and that beautiful thick black dick that he had watched take a piss probably fifteen or twenty times, but always soft and not excited. Today though, with his face up right close to it and with his eyes only about six inches from it, he did intend to see just how beautiful it was, when it was excited, stiff, and hard!

Jason stood there, now with his shorts and his briefs down around his ankles, his muscled bare chest feeling warm with the summer sun shining down on it, and his enlarged biceps hanging to his side, he looked down at David to ponder just what was going to happen next.

David stooped with his face directly in front of Jason's stick of meat, and he softly blew some warm air onto it. He watched silently as the crotch hair moved slightly. He took his hands off of his own knees and placed his left hand on Jason's right thigh, and his right hand on Jason's left thigh. He did hear Jason make a slight sigh as his hands reached their destinations. He liked what he heard. He knew Jason liked the feel of his hands touching his skin, although he was sure that, consciously, Jason did not know it. He knew that right then, Jason's mind was way off on too many other things.

Jason stood silently. David moved his face forward. He extended his tongue out and lightly touched the tip of Jason's uncut dick.

"David! David! I thought you were just gonna look at it! You said you just wanted to see it."

David looked up at his co-worker and replied, "No, Jason! Remember when I first asked, I told you I wanted to suck on it! I wanna suck it! I gotta man, I gotta!"

And with that statement, he lowered his face back down and immediately sucked all of Jason's dick into his mouth. It was then, but for not much longer, a soft dick! Almost immediately David could feel the growth of it, the stiffness of it and the strength of it, actually growing inside of his mouth. He heard Jason taking big long deep breaths!

David managed to slide the tip of his tongue in, under the foreskin, and as he did, he definitely knew Jason was 'there' and was emotionally getting into this! Consciously or not, he was getting into what was now happening to him and to his enormous dick! His dick was getting so stiff and so long that David could not keep his tongue inside of the cover. The dick was going too far back into the back of his throat, and licking the tip of it was now impossible! The other indication of Jason's favorable involvement was, Jason's hands, that were now on top of his head. He could feel Jason grabbing onto his scalp and moving his hands back and forth as if to silently be begging David to suck him off and suck him off good and hard!

All of a sudden, David realized that Jason was jerking at his left foot, as if trying to get his shorts off of his ankles. David pulled off of the oak tree rod, just long enough to reach down and pull Jason's shorts, and his briefs, off of his feet. Immediately he reached up and rather than grabbing onto the sides of Jason's thighs, he reached around and strongly grabbed onto each butt muscle. With his mouth immediately again taking all, of what had now become an eleven-inch dick, David felt Jason reposition his feet so that they were slightly farther apart and his stance was slightly more sturdy. Jason's hands were frantically roaming all over David's buzz cut, blonde head of hair.

"Oh, David! – Oh, David!! Oh David, suck on me man, suck on me! Oh my God man, suck on it man, suck on it! Oh man alive, this is so fucking good! Oh my God David, I've never felt anything like this before! Oh man suck it baby – suck on it! Oh, I've never been sucked on before man! I've never felt anything like this! Oh God man, I've never had my dick stuck in some guy's mouth before. Oh God man – oh shit, I am so fucking glad you're making me do this! Oh shit man – I never thought getting my dick sucked on would feel like this! Oh man what a wonderful feeling!! Oh my God I feel like I'm in heaven man, I do! Oh my God my dick feels so fucking good stuck in your mouth! Oh David, do it man – do it! Oh David, my dick is so fucking hard, it is so fucking hard! I don't think my dick's ever been this fucking hard man, I don't!! Oh man I can feel the back of your throat with my dick man – I can feel the tip of my dick all the way in the back of your throat! It's hitting your throat! Oh man, oh man! Do it man, do it! Oh my God man, I never thought getting sucked on could feel like this! Oh, do me man – do me! Suck me hard man – suck me hard!"

As David now had total, complete, unequivocal knowledge that his actions on Jason's dick were with total, and more than complete approval, he then loosed his left hand from Jason's right butt, quickly spit on his finger, threw his head back onto Jason's stick of meat, and after reaching around to Jason's backside, he slowly pointed his index finger in toward Jason's tight little, but sweet, asshole, and managed to slide most of his finger up and in, so that he could massage the inside of Jason as anxiously as he was now working on his dick. Jason knew he was getting finger fucked – his first time ever – and his body motions proved it. He was getting it on the dick and now up in the ass, and he liked it! He liked it, and he was trying to suck more and more finger up in there by tightening up his asshole just as tight as possible! He was letting David know that he liked it! He was giving all of himself to David now and he was actually begging for David to do even more!

David knew what Jason was doing, and he wanted to do as much to and for Jason that he could, so he pushed that finger, and a second one, up and into that hole, just as far as possible. He also knew that maybe – not right now – but hopefully before the camping trip was over, he was – maybe – going to get more than just a finger or two up in that hole! He wanted his dick poked up in there and then be able to go home knowing that he had finally gotten into the one asshole that he had been worshiping for six months now!

The approval 'ohhhs' and the 'ahhhs' that he heard Jason expressing, and the body motions that Jason was displaying, were showing some very, very, positive possibilities for some good deep ass action, a little later. The idea of maybe, just maybe getting to be lying on Jason, and fucking that beautiful, dark skinned, muscled ass was one hell of a lot more than David had ever hoped for. But right now, that was definitely looking like a true possibility! That ass was hungry, and David knew it! The way Jason was enjoying those two fingers up in there gave David the hopes that maybe putting his tongue up in there might be even that much more exciting and acceptable to Jason. He knew he sure was going to try and find out! He had watched that ass bend over so many times on the job and had visions of his face and that ass together, that maybe the day had finally come! He just knew that when he did it, he sure was not going to tell Jason what was happening! He wanted Jason to, just all of a sudden, realize that David had his face and his mouth in his ass! The way things were going now, David just knew that kind of action would totally turn Jason on, even more!

Somewhat as a surprise to David, Jason removed his left hand from on top of David's head, put it under his own bag of nuts and started squeezing it, rolling his nuts around, and pulling on it as he moved his right hand to the back of David's head, and strongly, and forcefully pulled it forward! His entire crotch was completely up against David's face! In-fact, as he looked down, he could not see David's face! As he looked down, that might have been his first, true realization that he now had every inch of his enormous, big, thick, black rod, rammed fully into his co-workers mouth. Suddenly he attempted to pull back as he almost yelled at David, "David, David you okay? David, David can you breathe?"

Without so much as pulling back off of the telephone pole that he now had very firmly planted way back past the back of his throat, David did manage to shake his head up and down slightly, to indicate that yes, he could breathe. He also grunted a slight, "Yeah."

With Jason now pulling David's head in toward his gut as tightly as possible, his own hand down below, pulling on his own bag of nuts, his leg muscles tightened up just about as tight as they could get, his butt muscles pulled in tight and solid, his legs spread wide, his stance now balanced up on his tip toes, and his head looking up toward the sky – if his eyes had been open – he started letting out some yells of excitement and sexual climax! He knew they were out in the wild, all by themselves, and he let it out – good and strong – just like some animal, out in the wild! He stood stiff and solid, and he grabbed onto David for support! He truly flooded David and all of David's insides with what felt like a full quart of cum! The hot, thick, protein cum that David had been praying for, ever since the day the company owner, Mr. Stanford, called him into the office, and introduced him to the new co-worker, Jason.

Nobody ever knew, nor had they ever been told, that as the new employee left Mr. Stanford's office that day, the owner looked over at David, grinned, winked, and quietly said, "Hey guy! I know what you like – definitely who you like it with, and I do remember just how you like it – so I assume you'll know how to take real good care of that man for as long as he works here. Make him happy! I hope you and he can become some very close co-workers. When I'm out of town, maybe he'll be a good substitute for me, and help you get things done. Help him learn

things from you, and then sometime you can show me what you
have taught him. Okay?"

"David, when you sucked me off earlier today, did you
swallow my cum? I gotta admit that when I let it fly, I assume
I had my dick in your mouth, but I gotta be honest man, I was
so fucking out of my mind right then, I'm not real sure of just
everything that was going on."

"Yeah Jason, yeah! You don't remember grabbing onto my
head and pulling my face up against you as tight as you could?"

"Yeah, well yeah kinda. David, when you first told me
what you wanted to do, I was so fucking freaked out that during
that entire time, I just kinda went a little crazy I guess, and yeah,
I gotta be honest, I just don't really remember how everything
went."

"It went good man, it went great!"

"Did I act like I liked it? Honestly man, I know it's weird,
but I guess my mind was so far out of it, I'm not sure of just how
I acted. You just sucked me off, right?"

"Well, yeah, sucked you off and did a little finger feeling
up in your asshole some."

"You what!? Finger feeling up in my asshole? You had a
finger up in my asshole?"

"Yes, yes! Honestly Jason, you don't remember me
feeling your asshole?"

"David – no I don't. Everything just kind of went fuzzy
for me when I got all excited once I saw my dick disappear down
your throat. I do remember thinking how no guy is supposed to
put his dick in some other guy's mouth, and how wrong everything

was that we were doing right then, but then, all of a sudden, my whole body just kind of went crazy and my mind really lost it. My body was feeling feelings like it never had before. I remember shooting off, but like I told you, I really did not remember if I was still stuck down in your throat or not, and of course, I didn't remember just where your hands were. David, I guess I finally got something that I just thought could never happen, but at the same time, I guess I had been wanting it to happen someway, with someone. Honestly man, do believe me, I'm not mad that you did that to me. Well – maybe I shouldn't say – 'to me' – cause I know I was part of it and I know I didn't try to fight you off. Do you think I really, internally, wanted that, even though I kinda kept saying 'No?'"

"Yes Jason – yes. I can't get in your mind and tell you how often you've looked at some guy and maybe wanted him to grab you and do you, but yes, I do think you had been wanting something like that to happen for probably a long time. You're a really hot looking, real well built, guy. I'm sure that over time you have had a lot of guys grabbing at you like I do, and you just never got mad at them, did you?"

"I guess maybe. Yeah, I've had some guys doing some stuff once in a while that I kinda wondered about, and yeah, I didn't get mad, but then I guess I just thought that whatever happened was all an accident."

"Like what happened? Tell me of some of the stuff that happened that you just blew off and ignored."

"Well – like about two years ago, I was taking a shower at the health club and this guy came up behind me and reached around me and grabbed my dick from behind, and when I turned around real fast and kinda asked what in the hell was going on, all of a sudden he tried to tell me that he thought I was some other guy, and he kind of apologized and said that he was sorry. I just said, 'Ok,' and let it go, but then I noticed that he kept looking at me and really didn't move away from me very fast. I thought that was kind of funny."

"Hey man, he was just praying that you'd, maybe, reach out and grab him. He didn't want to move away, hoping that you were agreeable and that you'd go for it. Were there just the two of you in the shower at that time? After that was over, did you maybe wish you had done something different?"

"I think I did – I honestly don't know. Yeah, it was just the two of us. I just remember that after he did move away from me and went to the other side of the room, I just kinda wished he had not moved so far away. But then I just went back to taking a shower and forgot about him."

"What else has happened that maybe later you kinda thought about?"

"One day just a few months ago, I was in the elevator in the Tower Hall Building downtown, and when the elevator stopped at one of the floors, and some people got in, the guy that was standing in front of me, he stepped back and at the same time, put his hands behind himself as if to grab onto his wrists, and when he did, I felt his hand hit my crotch. I think he actually slid the palm of his hand up and down the length of my cock. Of course the elevator was full and nobody could see what had happened, and I will admit to you right now, that I think I kinda leaned forward some as if to let him feel it more. That only happened for a couple of seconds, cause right then the elevator stopped again, and some of the people got off. We stood there, but not as close as we had been before they got off. I think he tried to move back up against me once, but I don't remember him touching me. He got off of the elevator before I did. I went on down to the ground floor."

"So how did you feel about him kinda sliding his hand up and down on your cock? Make you mad?"

"No, I guess not. Like I said, I kinda think I remember leaning forward some, so he could feel it some more, I guess. I think I was thinking, 'Well, if he wants to feel me out here in public, here man, feel it.' I know that if I did do that, or not, I just knew everybody was jammed so close together that nobody could see what he was doing. But then later I kept thinking about it, and then I wished that I had gotten off at the same floor as he did to just see if he'd say anything or maybe apologize. David, do you think I was actually wanting him to do it again?"

"Yes, emphatically, yes! Let me ask you something. What kind of clothes did you have on that day? What were you wearing?"

"I think I had on that pair of black and red running shorts that I wear once in a while, why?"

"Just as I thought! I figured you had something hot looking on that day. Jason, don't you realize that some Nun would want to reach out and grab you when you have those shorts, or your brown and tan shorts on. Jason, you wear those shorts without any jock strap, or briefs, on, and that stick of yours hangs down your left leg like it was a broken limb off of a big old oak tree. Hell man, how many times have I found some stupid reason to make a joke about something and then manage to reach out and try to grab that thing hanging in there? If you were downtown in the Tower Hall Building, what in the world were you doing in there wearing those sexy shorts?"

"My brother Jeremy works there on the 20th floor, and I had to take some papers down to him, for Mom."

"Holy shit man! Jason, don't you have any idea of what you are showing with those flimsy silky shorts on? I can understand you wearing 'em on the construction site, but to wear them downtown, in the Tower Hall Building, and obviously without a jock strap on, I'm surprised that nobody else tried to grab you. Or did they?"

"No, nobody else tried to grab me, but when I did get to the ground floor, some guy that I thought was going to get onto the elevator, for some funny reason turned around and stayed there in the lobby. When the doors came open, he was standing there all by himself, and I saw him looking at me, well I thought he was anyway, and then he just turned and did not get on the elevator. I could see him in the reflection of the window and he kept looking toward me until I opened the front door and left. I wondered why he kept looking my way, that whole time."

"I can tell you! He was hot and horny for what he could see. Jason, you make people hot and horny all the time. That is why I follow you to the restroom all of the time. Today is the first time I ever got to see it the way I wanted to see it, but man you'd better get used to people, guys and gals, and yes, nuns too, looking at that hunk of meat if you're gonna let it hang there and swing back and forth when you walk and wear those flimsy shorts."

"So David – you think I've been wanting something kinda like today to happen to me all along, even though I didn't know it?"

"Oh hell yes man, hell yes! The very first time you showed up at work wearing a pair of those flimsy shorts and your dick hanging down, flipping back and forth, I knew that day that you were gonna be game, but it took me until today to get us off together so I could finally get to it."

"David, how did you find out that you like to play with guys? How old were you?"

"I was just about your age, I was just shy of twenty one. I had been married for two years at the time. I was in Detroit at a meeting of some guys that went to a construction school together right out of high school. The school wanted us to come back for a three-day thing, to give the school an idea of how the school did as an instruction for us. Well – anyway, on the first night there, a bunch of us went out for some drinks, and we ended up in this "old out back trashy type of a bar." I think we went there cause we were not twenty one yet, and they would sell us beer. Anyway, as the night went on, and the beers went down, I was seated on a booth bench with this guy by the name of Rocky. I really don't think that was his real name, but that is what he went by, anyway! Yes, I admit, I got kind of snockered. Rocky got snockered too, but I really don't think as much as I did. But, I think he had his head on straight enough to get what he wanted, and what he wanted – was me!"

"All night long he kept sliding over closer and closer to me, and then he started putting his hand on my shoulder, then down on my leg, then eventually on my crotch. At first I moved it back over toward him, for a few times, but then I guess I didn't care anymore, cause I let him keep it there. There were a few comments made from somebody there at the table that made us all laugh and when we did, then his hand just kinda, for some reason or another, grabbed onto my leg tighter, and tighter, and then finally onto my crotch when I had quit moving it. Like I said, after a while, his touching me didn't matter, and I guess I was liking it, or I would have made him stop. I mean, after all, he was the hottest looking thing that had ever touched me, my entire life. His touching me kind of reminded me of the days on the football field, and having the other big guys touching me. So I guess maybe that's the reason that his touching me didn't really bother me too much."

"Yes, he was a black man, about twenty three or twenty four years old. He was just a little older than the rest of us, and I think he was the one that knew where we, the younger ones, could buy beer. He stood about six foot three or four, muscles on body parts, "that most people don't even have." I mean muscles, muscles and muscles. He competed in a lot of body building events – so I kinda remember him saying, anyway. Hell, he might have just said that, so that I'd get all hot and bothered for him. If so, he sure didn't need to show, or say, anything more than that body, to make anybody hot and bothered. Gotta remember, I was pretty well snokered that night. Well, that is until later that night when I really came out of it, real fast."

"When you really came out of it? What do you mean? How?"

"It finally hit closing time, and the bar had to close. We called a cab, and we all piled into it and headed back to the hotel where we were staying. There were six of us all together. So all of us in one cab, it got crowded. I ended sitting on top of Rocky's lap. He managed to keep ahold of me the entire ride, saying he didn't want me to slide off. He hung onto me mostly by grabbing my crotch. Part of the time, he'd kind of hide his hand, the one that he was grabbing my crotch with, by laying his other arm across it. Some of the other guys that were in the back seat noticed it and made comments about it, but he just laughed it off saying, 'Well, I gotta put my hand somewhere. It's kinda crowded in here.' Those guys did not know that he had been grabbing some part of me, somewhere, during almost the entire time at the bar. And most of that time, it was grabbing on my crotch. Hell, by that time, I didn't care any, and maybe I was actually enjoying the attention."

"We got to the hotel, and Rocky insisted on paying for the cab, which meant that we, yeah 'we,' had to kinda hang back some and let the other guys go ahead and go to their rooms. Rocky kept ahold of me after the cab stopped, and wouldn't let me leave when the other guys did. He paid for the cab, then almost as if under arrest, he walked me to his room. He kept telling me that I was way too drunk to be left alone, and besides he was not sure I would be able to find my room. I guess I didn't fight back any."

"We went into his room, and before he got undressed, he laid me down on the bed, and then stripped me bare. At first I didn't know if I liked him getting me all undressed, but then, you gotta remember, I was snockered and not really thinking too clearly. I remember, that for one short moment while lying there, for a minute I thought I was at the coach's house, and that Rocky was my old football coach. I guess I must have had some secret desires for Coach John, that I just never realized until that few short seconds lying there all naked, and watching Rocky. I laid there and watched him start taking his clothes off. The first thing to come off was his polo shirt. He grabbed the bottom of it, pulled it up over his head, and I think I immediately went into shock. What a gorgeous, gorgeous body! I could of course, see his arms even with the shirt on, but when he pulled that up and off of his head, and exposed that monument of a chest, I almost lost it! That is when I came back to life! His mahogany skin, pulled across his back and his chest was a picture beyond belief. I had seen some bodybuilding magazines before, but I had never seen anything as hot as this site was. If I did know that I should not be there – that I should grab some pants and run – my mind could not do it. Right then, somebody could have yelled 'fire,' and there is no way that I could have jumped up and run. I was speechless, and I was motionless. Right then, I was helpless."

"Rocky bent over and removed his shoes, then unbuckled his pants, slid them down and just like you, wore nothing under his pants, except for the longest, thickest, stiffest most beautiful black cock that any man has ever owned. All of a sudden I wanted to cry knowing that for hours, at the bar, that man, and that dick were sitting right beside me, and while he was playing around with my crotch, I could have – could have! – been feeling what he was now showing. For hours, I could have had that dick in my hand, and I could have been feeling the strength of it, the length of it, and the girth of it, if I had only known! I laid there on the bed, and for the very first time in my life, I felt my cock rise up and salute a man looking at it. Never before had I ever gotten excited about any other man, his dick, his body, or anything he had ever said to me, that might have been a 'come-on.'"

"Rocky turned toward the dresser, bent over and removed his pants. His ass, aimed directly at my face. Never before in my entire life had I ever seen another man's asshole. Slowly, Rocky reached around, one hand on each cheek, grabbed ahold of each cheek, and pulled the crevice of his ass apart. Now, less than two feet in front of me, I saw a sight that has never left my mind! I was lying there looking at a part of Rocky that even he – himself – had never seen. I had used and heard the comment, 'Oh eat my ass,' so many times, and I thought it was just some nasty saying, but right then I wanted to do it, and do it with a lot of love. I had never, ever, thought that at any time of my life I would ever think that 'Eat my ass,' could actually be considered as an actual act. Right then, I understood it could be, and why it could be. It was beautiful! It was solid! It was a site that could not be described in words! I wanted him to just sit down on my face. I wanted to eat it, one slow bite at a time. Slowly Rocky stood back up. He turned toward me, grinned and asked, 'Like what you see?' I laid there completely stunned. Shocked, stunned, and unbelievably horny for doing something – anything – but yet something, with this statue of a man. A man that had presented himself to me so splendidly and with so much royalty. I had never lusted nor even remotely thought about doing anything with another man – that is until then!! I had a bronze God lying down in bed beside me, and I was at his grateful mercy."

"I was at his absolute and total control. I could not fight off any actions that, for some funny old reasons, I used to think were all wrong. On that night, anything he wanted, anything he suggested, anything he did, was a gift to me from heaven."

"He stood there, looking down at me, grinning at me, apparently somehow knowing and aware that I had never been in bed with another man before, and he silently bent down, slid his tongue from my Adams apple, down the full length of my chest, to my fuzzy crotch, then slid his hands under each side of my ass cheeks, opened his mouth, and suddenly took my entire stiff rod into his mouth. All of a sudden, I was being sucked on, and enjoyed by a man, in his bed, without him ever having mentioned sex, or the possibility of the action of having sex. Never, at the bar, during the cab ride home, nor even as we entered the room, had the subject or word of sex come up, but yet, there I was, totally bare, with a raging hard-on standing up as if it was a flagpole, in the hotel room of a man that I had just met hours earlier. A man that any and every bodybuilding magazine would pay enormous amounts of money to have on their cover. A man, that had not even slightly mentioned sex, a man that had displayed his most private of spots in a very pronounced, 'look at me type of action,' and was now lying beside me just as bare as any small child or animal, at the time of birth. This man was now sucking my heterosexual cock – or so I had always thought it was – and I had no thoughts nor desires to attempt any stop. Internally I was yelling for more, harder, deeper and thank you man, thank you! I had not yet spoken a word. The entire time in his hotel room, I had been completely silent, and fully stunned at all of the sights and the feelings that I was experiencing. Everything was a completely new and stunning experience. Never before, in my entire life, had I every been so awe struck, that I was powerless. Never before had I ever lusted for even the idea of having sex with another man, and right then, I would have fought off any attempt, or anything, or any person, that wanted it to stop. I was sorry and remorseful that our companionship could not have been out in the open, in the middle of a major city park, so that any and every person within miles could see me living a life of sexual excitement that I had never dreamt of as ever being a possibility. I thought that I had experienced some magnificent sex before, and especially since I was one of the high school football stars and could get any girl anytime I wanted, but nothing, absolutely nothing, even started to compare with the feelings and emotions that I was experiencing with him right then."

"Oh David, I can't believe it. Did you stay with that guy all night, then?"

"Yeah, sure did. My whole life changed that night. My getting sucked off and having his hands underneath my butt and feeling him squeeze my butt cheeks, was just the beginning of that night."

"Wait, wait! Just the beginning? What happened. Did you do more stuff?"

"Oh yeah, sure did. He sucked me off, then he turned me over and massaged my back and butt like I had never felt before. I told you about how I saw his asshole and how I wanted to eat it? Well, that is exactly what happened to mine. While he had me lying there on my gut, and he was rubbing my back and my butt, he pulled my cheeks apart and pushed his face up in there, and then started roaming around up in there with his tongue. Oh man, I almost went crazy! I had never felt anything like that in my life before! I had rubbed my ass cheeks before with my hands, like washing 'em, but I sure as hell had never had a face and a tongue up in there, but I sure did that night. Damn, it felt good!"

"David, you mean he actually put his face up in your ass? Is that what you're saying?"

"Yeah, yeah. Jason, I'm gonna tell you, it's a feeling like you've never had before. I'm gonna be honest with you man, real honest, I wanna do that to your ass. Can I?"

"Oh shit man, I don't know. Guys aren't supposed to do that to each other, are they?"

"Hey, only if they want to! I'm telling you, I want to, and now all I need is for you to tell me that you want to see what it's like. Can I?"

"Oh shit man, you're starting to make me wonder what it's like. David, I've always been told guys are not supposed to play with other guys, doing stuff like that! I think I want to, but I've always been told doing something like that is all wrong."

"And it is all wrong for what reason? If I want to do it, and you want to do it, or maybe I should say, have it done to you, what is wrong? All you need to do is drop those shorts you've got on, bend over there on that log, give me your ass, and just feel something that you've never felt before. You're sure not gonna get hurt any, and nobody else is ever gonna know we did it, unless you tell 'em, so it's up to you."

And stating that, David simply sat there and looked at Jason as if asking, 'Well? Wanna do it or not?'

Slowly Jason stood up, tucked his thumbs under this waistband. Slowly started pulling the waist band down, looked at David, and said, "I still don't know if I should be doing this or not, but now I'm afraid that if I don't let you do it, then maybe I'm gonna wonder for a long time if I should have, and I'm gonna wonder what it could have felt like. So yeah! Come on, let's do it. I just hope I don't regret it!"

Jason stripped off his shorts, and as he did, David was very pleasantly surprised to see that Jason had been very successfully hiding a hard-on, and as he stepped out of the shorts, he did bend over a large log, and David moved in behind.

Jason hung his head as if to think, "If I don't look, then I won't know what is happening." He felt David move in behind himself, and he felt David put a hand on each butt cheek.

Softly and slowly, David moved his face forward, and let the tip of his nose start the entry into Jason's ass crevasse. Softly David slid his hands around each cheek and starting to pull them apart. Blowing a small amount of warm air in toward Jason's hole, David managed to move in closer and closer. Suddenly Jason felt the tip of David's tongue reach his hole and he immediately uttered an, "Oh yeah, oh yeah! Oh my God David! You've got your tongue in my hole don't you? You've got your tongue up in there don't you?"

David managed a slight, "Yeah," but his action of moving his head up and down in response was much more successful.

Within the next ten minutes, Jason lost all hesitations as to why his ass should not be licked and poked with the tip of a tongue, and more than once, he begged David to, "Push harder man, push harder! Tongue it man – tongue it! Oh my God David, I can't believe you are actually back there eating on my ass! Oh my God it feels so good!"

As David tucked his tongue back into his mouth, he pulled his face back out of the ass crevasse and allowed Jason's butt cheeks to go back to their normal position, he slightly tapped Jason on the butt and said, "You've just had your ass eaten out man. You cannot say, that nobody has ever eaten that chocolate cookie out. Thanks Jason, thanks."

Kinda shaking his head some, and at the same time squeezing his ass cheeks together some, and at the same time grabbing onto his own hard-on, Jason slowly stood back up, and asked, "So why are we so told that doing something like that is all bad? Oh man, what a great feeling! David, I'm sorry I've acted so 'skimish' about doing stuff. I don't know what I've been thinking. Why are we told that we're not supposed to be doing that stuff? So far you've given me a blow job, and you've given me an ass eating, and both of them have felt fantastic, and maybe I'm stupid for asking this, but, what else do you wanna do? Oh God man, should I be asking that?"

"Hey man, if you're asking, I'm telling. I want that enormous rod of yours up in my butt! Like I told you earlier, I only play with black men, and it's because of rods like yours that I'm particular. I sure as hell do not want to go home from this campout without getting that long thing poked up into my butt, as far as you can ram it. Every time I've taken a piss beside you, my mind has just plain gone wild wishing I could just, right then, bend over, spread my ass and tell you to slam it. I do not want to go home without knowing that I got that up in my ass at least once."

"Okay, I can do that, I'm sure. I've never fucked some guy's ass before, but after what you've shown me so far, fucking a tight asshole has gotta be a pretty damn good thing too! When we gonna do that?"

"Let's clean up this campsite some, get the dishes washed up, set a small fire, throw some blankets out here on the ground, and then I want you to poke me here by the fire."

"I'm gonna fuck you out here in the open? Should we do that?"

"Hey, it's private. I camp out here with my buddies all the time, and the only people that I've ever seen out here are my buddies. And besides that, nobody's gonna be out here walking around after dark, anyway."

After getting the campsite somewhat tidied up and the camping dishes washed, the blankets thrown down, and a small fire started, Jason stripped off his shorts, laid down and then asked, "Do you and your buddies fuck each other out here?"

"Oh yeah, all the time. This is kinda of our secret hiding place when we decide we need some good ole guy-to-guy sex, and we need a place away from the wives."

"You've never had anybody come wondering by, while you were camping out here?"

"Well, just once. Just one time."

"Somebody did come by? Was everything okay? I mean, you weren't in the process of having sex were you?"

"Well, yeah after a little while, everything was okay. It was a Saturday afternoon and we had a group of about six guys out here. Everything had been pretty quiet ever since we had gotten here the day before, and since it was then afternoon, we really did not expect to see anybody else come in and set up camp, but they did. Three guys came in, and they kinda heard us some. All six of us, we were rather active with each other, and making a little more noise than maybe we should have, and one of those guys happened to hear us and started over toward our campsite, that is until he got close enough to see what was happening. I guess he stood there for a little while, then he went back and told his buddies what he had found. They came over and tried to make some trouble, but, from what I could figure out, one of them was anxious for a blow job, but his buddies apparently did not know he was into gay sex, so anyway, he was the one that suggested that if we would give each one of them a blow job, they'd keep their mouths shut. So we agreed, and each of us six, gave each one of them a blowjob. That pretty well took up the rest of the afternoon. That's the only time I've ever sucked a white dick. All three of those guys were white guys, so I didn't have any choice.

The guy that made the initial comment about us sucking 'em off, to keep 'em from saying anything, did seem to be the guy that enjoyed everything the most. He had the first hard-on when we got started, and his dick was still hard when we finally got done. I think he wanted to camp with us instead of with his own buddies. The next day, he showed up over here, for no reason at all, a couple of times. Always acting like he needed something, but what I really think he was wanting was some phone numbers. We didn't give him any, since everybody in our group was married guys, and we did not need some horny single guy messing things up for us at home."

Listening to David tell about the time that the other three did come across their campsite, Jason kept looking around and then asked, "You sure nobody's around here tonight? We're out here by the fire and I'm gonna be fucking you in the ass. I don't want somebody coming by and seeing us doing it. You sure it's okay out here?"

"Yeah, yeah. Hey that one time was a real abnormal thing. Honestly, I think that time, those guys were out here because that one guy was hoping to maybe get them into some sex stuff, so he picked the way out of the way campsite. He seemed to kind of be the ring leader. He was the one that kind of told the others what to do. He was the anxious one of the lot. The others just did what he said, and I'm not so sure either one of them had ever had his dick sucked on before. This spot is way too far off of the beaten path for somebody to come in, especially this late in the day."

With that explanation, Jason said, "Oh, okay. If you say so."

After getting Jason rather calmed down, and not acting quite so nervous about doing the fucking out in the open, David then told him, "Hey man, come over here and let me get some greasy stuff on that rod of yours. Unless we want everybody in the main campgrounds hear me yelling in pain, we'd better get your cock and my ass really coated with some good slippery grease, so that you don't tear my ass up and wide open, when you poke it in."

Within moments David had coated Jason's cock and smeared some lube up into his asshole, and then laid face down and told Jason, "Go to it man, fuck me! I wanna feel you up inside of me! Fuck me."

Taking Jason's thick eleven-inch rod very quickly and without comment, Jason then asked, "David, I went up in you all the way with just one push, and you never said anything. You didn't even groan any. Do you get fucked so often that you don't even act like something is happening back here anymore?"

Turning his head so that he could talk to Jason, David replied, "When it feels this fucking good, why make an issue out of it. Yeah, I felt it, and it felt damn good, and it still does, so I just figured, why make an issue out of something that is so damn good? Seriously man, whenever I do get fucked by some guy, it is always with a big dick, or I'm just not interested. Ever since I saw your dick the very first time, my ass has been waiting and waiting for it, and I am just plain enjoying what I've been waiting for, for way too long. Poke me man, poke me! Tonight is your chance to see what fucking some guy's ass is like, and it's your chance to get rough and rowdy back there. Fucking some guy is a lot different than fucking some gal. A guy's ass likes it good and rough, and so tonight is your chance to really find out what giving someone a good rough fuck is like. Do it to me! Take your opportunity to get really rough back there. When you get back home, you're gonna have to go slow and easy with the fucking there again. Poke me man, poke me! Ram my ass! Slam your dick in me and find out what one hell of a good rough fucking can feel like!"

Without any further talking or instructions, Jason did as he was told. He pounded David's ass harder and stronger than he had ever thought a person could get fucked. But then, all of a sudden he realized that, yes, he was fucking a man now, and not some soft bodied woman. He was in one hell of a strong body that was strong, solid, and begging for some good strong, solid action. He went to it. He decided to see if he could actually get David to plead for some easier, slower comfort, or was he the one that was going to have to admit that he was now out of energy, and that he had to stop.

Ten minutes went by, eleven minutes went by, twelve minutes went by and Jason was still pounding up and down on, and in and out of David's ass as fast and as hard as he could. Finally, he did have to admit that he was needing to slow down some, and he did admit that he thought he would be able to get David to ask for some easier action, but he also had to admit that he simply could not fuck David long enough, hard enough, nor rough enough to get him to say, "Stop."

Clasping completely down onto David, Jason managed to say, "Oh shit man, how much can you take? God man, I'm fucking exhausted! David, you okay? I thought I was beating the hell out of you. How long can you get fucked like that? Man, I'm exhausted!"

Sounding as if maybe he was completely exhausted too, David turned his head toward Jason, and said, "I just got fucked rougher, harder and longer than any fucking I've ever received, but there was no way in hell that I was gonna tell you to stop. I was finally getting what I've been praying for, for years, and there was no way I was gonna tell you I had to stop. Seriously man, while you were pounding on me, I decided that if I did go home with black and blue marks on my ass, and if I did have trouble trying to walk right, I'd just have to make up some excuses, cause

I was finally getting what I had been looking for, and there was no way I was gonna tell you I had to stop. Jason, you are the man that I have been looking for, ever since I got that first big rod of Rocky's pushed up in my ass! You okay man? You alright? Do you know now, why I only get fucked by black men with great big dicks on 'em? When I get fucked, it's gotta be one hell of a big thick strong stiff dick, and a man attached to it that really knows how to beat and pound an ass. Jason, you are my man! You've got the dick, and believe me man, you sure as the hell know how!"

Now, with a smile across his face, Jason looked at David and said, "Well, all I can say right now is that you've got one hell of a hot ass. When I found out why you had us come up here, I thought I was kinda pissed since I thought maybe you fooled me, but David, I just wish we could have been doing this stuff a lot sooner. Hell, maybe I should have done some of this stuff before I got married. I'm exhausted, after fucking your ass like that, but I gotta fuck you some more so that I can cum. I'll go slow and easy, but man, if I don't let it fly, it's gonna keep me awake all night long. I've got me too much juice built up in there to try and go to sleep on. Get your ass ready man, my big black rod – as you like to refer to it – is coming back in."

And under some very different modes of action now, this time good and slow, and with a lot of emotions, Jason did take advantage of the 'one hell of a hot ass,' as he had just referred to it.

Without hurry, and without rush, Jason took advantage of the first man's ass that he had ever experienced, and he enjoyed it immensely. And even while he was still well embedded, using the full length of his admired, 'big long black swinging rod,' as David had referred to it, he made sure that he did get a firm declared statement from David, that this fucking was definitely not going to be the only time that he ever got to use this ass. He had found something that he liked! He wanted to hear a very firm stated commitment that, at least once a month, as long as they knew each other, that this, 'My dick in your ass,' would continue.

    And it did. David and Jason worked together for the next three years, and on schedule, with the minimum of at least once a month, they managed to find themselves as the last two people at the company that day, and then the recently remodeled employee lunchroom and lounge room was well taken advantage of. The lounge room did include a day bed, intended for use if an employee needed someplace to lie down, for a moment. David and Jason did find it very convenient to use, for more than just a moment. With the convenience of that day bed, Jason did get the opportunity to re-enter the hottest little white ass that he had ever seen. And yes, over those three years, David did anxiously take advantage of the hot, black, strong and solid ass, that Jason so proudly carried around each day. Jason's being 'so proud of it,' was a learning experience. It did take David about a year to help Jason truly understand, just what a beautiful ass, he was carrying around, for everybody to see. But finally one day, Jason did finally admit that maybe, just maybe, his ass was a hell of a lot hotter looking than the other guys that he had recently been checking out. It was a year after that eventful day, when he went camping with David, that he did have any realization of what a golden prize he carried around with himself, each and every day.

    His realization of just how hot of a body he did have, never occurred to him until that hot July afternoon, at the company picnic/swimming party. That day, he did look over the other 'stock' of the company, as he and David did refer to the other men of the company, and definitely did notice that almost everybody there, men, women, and even including Mr. Stanford, did act as if they were paying a little more attention to him, and his tight fitting – crotch hugging – and ass kissing Speedos, than he had ever noticed before. He knew that it had been David's constant positive comments about his body that finally made him be aware of the attention he was receiving.

It was not until the very last day on the job – before Jason moved on to another city and a new opportunity – that he was finally told how and why Mr. Stanford had hired him – so quickly – when they met face to face. David confided in him, that Mr. Stanford, too, had admired that tight, solid, bubbled ass – from the first day – the day when he came in for his interview.

Knowing of all of the actions and sessions that had happened, and had been going on for the past three years – but yet never letting Jason be aware of the activities, and the secret sessions that he and David had also been having – Mr. Stanford shook hands with Jason, and emphatically thanked him for all of the great work that he had done for the company, and for all of his co-workers, and especially how he had spent the time working with David, and offering all of his assistance and good help, to David. As they shook hands for the final time, Mr. Stanford did say, "Jason, thank you from all of us. We have been very fortunate to have had you working here, and I know I can speak especially for David. I know you have been an especially close, co-worker of his. Thank you, and I wish you the best of luck wherever you go, and in whatever you do. You have a lot to offer, wherever you are, and with whomever you are with, and you certainly did prove that while you were here with us. All of us are very sorry to see you go, and later – when you are gone – we will be very sorry that you are gone. Especially, David and I will have some very fond memories of you, and having you here, and what you have done for us. Take care and be safe."

In the parking lot, as David stood beside the open door of Jason's car, and as Jason was getting himself positioned to drive, he did look up at David and ask, "Hey guy. This morning you told me that Mr. Stanford had checked out my ass the day he hired me, and that he liked it too. How did you know that? Then – just now – he made the comment about how he knew how close of a co-worker you had been, and how he and you will have very fond memories of what I have done for you. What did he mean by that? Why did he say that? Does Mr. Stanford know what we've been doing, for the past three years? Does he know we've been screwing each other? Do you and he get together too?"

Looking at Jason, David smiled and then stated, "Jason, I've had my opportunities to meet and greet some pretty good people, and I will always classify you as the one, on the top of the quality list! Mr. Stanford liked what he saw – he knew I was gonna like what I saw too – and Mr. Stanford knew he was hiring someone that was gonna be very important to me – and especially, when he was out of town, or busy. He was taking a chance making that move, but as we all found out, it was a very smart move, and it worked out for all of us just the way we wanted it to. But when he hired you, he just didn't know how important you would became to me. Everything just went way beyond him just trying to make sure I had company – some good strong black company, if you know what I mean – when I needed it. He knew I was thinking about maybe leaving the company back then, and he wanted me to stay with the company, and he also knows that I need some occasional help, in finding the right kind of a person, to work really close to, and to get really close to. When you came in, he took one look at you and he knew how valuable you could be to the whole operation. After our little camping session together, I asked that the lunch and lounge rooms be re-furbished, and he knew why. He knew why we needed a day bed in there. Hiring you, kept me with the company. I will now have to 'make due' with what I used to use, and without you, I will now be back to using the original cast of characters, which I call the 'old stock.' Mr. Stanford will now just have to keep his eyes open for the right kind of a replacement, to take your place. Your place – in a couple of different ways. He's had a couple of very happy co-workers working together, for the past three years, and I know he wants that to happen again. Jason, take care! I will miss you very much! Very much!"

And with that statement made, David reached in, patted Jason on the chest, closed the car door, and then very solemnly said, and waved, "Good-bye."

One Hot Coach!

Tony was built big – built strong – was really, really muscled – had a sharp looking black shaved head, and obviously was built like a brick shithouse! Arms to lock onto – whenever possible – and legs that should have been on a quarter horse! Looked just like what he was – a college football coach. And he was one hot coach! He truly was one of those guys that gay guys – well others too probably – drooled over whenever he was shown on TV during one of the Saturday afternoon games. And he was on, often enough, and long enough, to where gays all over the area wondered just who was on the camera, and just *why* was he shown so often? Their thinking – "One hot and hungry gay camera man!"

Tony sat down on a big rock that was close to the trail, and attempted to rather re-group from his fast-paced hike up to the top of the hill, and then partway back down. He was sipping from his water bottle and taking deep breathes when rather all of a sudden, he had company.

"Oh, Hi! Where in the hell did you come from?" Tony asked, as the young man, looking to be about maybe twenty-three or twenty-four, stepped up, extended his right hand out for a handshake and said, "Hi! I'm Chris, how you doing?"

As Tony remained seated and Chris stepped closer to shake hands, he replied, "Oh, I was over there. There, by that big bunch of bushes. There's a nice lookout over there that you can't see from here, and unless you know about it, it's real easy to go past and never know it."

"Really? Really? What does it look out over? Over the valley?"

"Yeah, yeah it does. Come on, wanna see it? I'll show you how to find it."

Figuring, 'Hey, why not? Might be something to see,' Tony stood up and followed the young man down a slight path.

After kinda ducking into and under some bushes, and some branches, they did approach an open spot that did have a great view of the valley floor down below. It took an additional walk of about a hundred feet or more before the two reached the greatest view, where they stopped and silently for a minute or two, just looked.

"Nice isn't it?" Tony rather softly asked.

"Yeah." Was the even more softly answered reply.

Now looking over at his new companion, Tony looked at him, and away from the view, due to Chris's very quiet reply of, "Yeah," which did sound rather limp. Tony turned and looked at Chris, to realize that Chris was not looking at the view, well the valley view anyway, but rather at his crotch and his legs.

"Uhhh – what you doing man?"

"Oh, I'm sorry, I'm sorry! You've been hitting the trail pretty heavy today haven't you? You been hiking it pretty fast, right?"

Totally confused as to just what in the hell was now going on, Tony did reply, "Well yeah, I guess so. Why? Why'd you ask that?"

Looking up at Tony and then really taking a big deep breath and looking as if he was bracing himself, Chris then quietly added, "You're all sweaty! You're sweaty! I like that! I like the way you smell."

"What, what in the hell did you just say?"

"I like the way you smell. I like that! I like that smell."

"What in the hell are you doing man? What are you doing?" Tony strongly asked as he watched Chris lick his lips and almost stare at his sweaty, sweat sparkling chest."

"Hey man, hey! Hey I'm not gonna touch you man, but can I smell you? Can I!? I won't touch you. Okay? Can I?"

Now really confused and shocked, not really disappointed in what he was hearing though, Tony finally said, "Well – I guess you are now, aren't you? You can smell me can't you?"

"Yeah, but I wanna smell your crotch man, can I please, please!!?"

"Smell my crotch!?" Tony almost let out as a yell. "Smell my crotch!? Why in the hell do you wanna smell my crotch?"

Now looking directly at Tony and really taking some deep breathes, Chris answered, "I know man, I know! It's weird, I know that, but I like to smell a hot and sweaty man's crotch. Especially a big strong man like you. Please, please, I promise I won't touch you, I just wanna get down there in front of it and smell it good and deep. You don't have to do anything, just stand there or maybe sit over there on that log and just let me put my face up close there and smell it. Okay, please man, please!?"

Stunned and now shocked, Tony didn't know what to say, or do, so he just said, "Okay. Yeah, if you want to, I guess so."

Without giving Tony any chance to change his mind, Chris immediately stooped down in front of Tony, and came within about two inches of Tony's crotch and sniffed and sniffed deeply. "Oh yeah man, oh yeah! Oh man, I love the way you smell! I love it, I love it!"

Chris continued to squat there, his hands on his own legs acting as support, and his face pushed out as far as he dared to go, and he sniffed Tony's sweaty body and his male area, crotch.

Stepping back just a step, Tony said, "Hey guy. Here, let me sit down on the log so I can spread my legs out some. If you really wanna sniff my crotch that much, I might as well get my legs opened up some so you can get in there and enjoy it. Why – why in the hell you do, and why you'd want to, I'll never know, but hey, if you want to, I guess it's just you and me back here, so go for it."

Tony did sit down on the log, spread his legs out wide, and rather presented his crotch to Chris, to move into and sniff. And Chris did! He positioned himself so that he had his face nicely positioned right up as close to Tony's crotch as possible, but without touching him. He had made a promise, and he was sticking to his guns.

Tony was just shocked. He had never had some guy, even come so close, to doing something so weird. He sat there, his arms stretched back behind himself supporting his weight as he sat there and watched Chris sniff and sniff at his crotch and his legs. Tony did not suggest he do anything more than sniff and look. Tony had not given Chris the okay to touch his skin. At least three times though, Chris moved in toward Tony's crotch so close that Tony thought Chris was probably gonna put his mouth on it, but he never did. Once, Tony actually thought he was going to, and even though he didn't want to admit it to himself, let alone to Chris, he was kind of disappointed that it never happened.

For a bewildering second there, he actually wondered if he had wanted Chris to do it, and maybe bite on it some. He realized that for a second there, he had actually had a moment of anxiety about that happening, and that was a very good and positive anxiety. He had never had that feeling enter his head before, at any time, and he was now a thirty four year old man. That was definitely a very weird feeling to have experienced.

After probably four or five minutes of Chris moving his head up and down the length of Tony's long muscular legs, and of course up and as close to, as possible, to his crotch, he finally sat up, smiled at Tony and emphatically said, "Thank you man, thank you! I know you think that is weird, but I know people do weirder things than smell someone, and when I saw you on the trail earlier, I just knew I had to see if I could do it! Thanks man, thanks!"

"Uhh, okay guy, okay! I mean I guess – okay! If that's something that turns you on, I guess it was okay with me."

"Hey man, I really do appreciate it, I do! You come hiking up here very often?"

"No. No. I just checked into the lodge this morning, so this is the first time I've even hiked this area. You come up here often?"

"The lodge!? You staying at the lodge? You staying at Byridge Lodge?"

"Yeah, yeah. Yeah, me and my wife. We're gonna be here till Sunday."

"Oh shit man. Oh man, I wait tables there! Oh shit, you'll be seeing me there."

"You do!? You a waiter in the dining room?"

"Yeah, oh crap man, oh shit! Please, please don't tell anyone what I did today – please!"

"Hey guy, no problem, no problem. You really think I want my wife finding out I sat here and let a guy run his nose up and down the insides of my legs and up against my crotch? I don't think so! I mean man, I'm just as thankful that you don't want anyone knowing anything either! I mean, how in the hell could I explain this to her?"

"Oh man, oh shit. Uhhh, oh shit man, I don't know your name man, but please help me keep my weird ways a secret! I'd get fired if somebody found out!"

"Hey, cool man, cool. Nobody's gonna find out anything. Believe me man, nobody. So that you don't accidentally call me by name, let's just go by Coach. Okay? Everybody knows me as 'Coach,' and if by accident you say something to me in the lodge, nobody's gonna think anything funny if you happen to call me Coach."

"Yeah, yeah, okay."

"So Chris, you come up here often?"

"Well yeah, I guess I do. I do kinda – cause of my funny weird stuff. I can usually find someone up here that understands my funny stuff, but course, not somebody as hot as you. So, I gotta guess you are a coach someplace, since you said everybody calls you coach, right?"

"Yeah, yeah. I'm a university assistant coach, but tell you what! Since you don't recognize me from being on TV with my team, let's just not worry about it. You, maybe, not knowing just who I am, might be better. So, when you gonna be hiking this hill again?"

"Probably tomorrow. Yeah, probably tomorrow. WHY!? Why? You wanna be here again? Is that why you asked? Oh my God man! You wanting to meet me here again? Really – really!?"

"Hey Chris, you sure didn't do anything to me that I can complain about, and yeah, I will admit having some guy sniff around on my crotch and legs like that was not real sickening, so yeah, I'd agree to let you smell me again tomorrow. Why not? Hey man, your nose and my crotch, why not?"

"Oh Coach, oh really? Really!? You'd let me do that again?"

"Hey man, no harm done is there? I know it might be kinda funny, but hey, I didn't mind you running your face up in there and smelling me. Not so sure I'd wanna do it, but hey, if it turns you on, why not? Nothing wrong with that is there?"

"No, no I don't think so."

"So tell me man. Smelling a guy's crotch. What other funny stuff you into? Wait a minute, I shouldn't be using the word 'funny.' Maybe what's funny to me isn't to everybody else. What other stuff do you like to do? Not saying I'd agree to doing something, but gotta admit, I kinda find it interesting to see just what some other guy finds interesting and exciting."

"Oh Coach, Coach. I'm afraid to tell you man, I'm afraid you wouldn't wanna know me then."

"Hey man, why not? I'm not slamming you for smelling me and my crotch, so why do you think I'd think bad about other stuff? Okay, so tell me what? What else you like?"

"Uhhh Coach, if we meet tomorrow, can you maybe wear some briefs or a jock strap that I can take home with me? Can you do that?"

"Take home with you!? Why? Why would you want to take home my briefs or my jock strap?"

"Cause I wanna have 'em at home to smell."

"Oh!? Have 'em at home to smell!? Is that what you want? You wanna take my smelly dirty underwear or jock strap home and throw your nose in it? Right?"

"Yeah, yeah. And maybe I can get you to piss in 'em before you take 'em off and give 'em to me? Maybe?"

"Hey man, deal! I got some jock straps that I've worn while I was coaching some of the games, and hey, if that's a turn on to you, why not? I'll make sure I drink a lot of water during my hike so I really gotta take a good long piss when I get done. Okay? That what you want guy?"

"Yeah man, yeah! Oh yes! Oh Coach, this is fucking turning me on man, this is turning me on! Thanks man, thanks! I've never found me a guy that understands me like you do! Usually they get all pissed at me and tell me I'm just fucking crazy! Oh Coach, thanks! So, like can we meet here the same time tomorrow? Don't let anybody see you sneak in here behind the bushes. I don't what anybody else here but us. Okay? Oh man, I'm gonna get to smell your dirty underwear or jock right? Hey man, what you got on right now? Briefs or a jock?"

"I've got a jock strap on right now. Want me to pull my shorts down so you can see it and smell it some right now?"

"Oh would you!? Oh man, can I? Oh Coach, yeah man, yeah!"

Coach did pull his running shorts down slightly, and Chris wasted no time in getting his nose in there and right up close. He breathed in three deep breathes, then said, "Oh Coach! Coach, can you keep this strap on maybe all the time until tomorrow so I can smell it again then? It'll really, really smell like you then! Can you do that?"

"Chris, I don't see why not! Course I can't wear it to bed. I sleep naked and my wife would wonder just what in the hell was going on if I left it on at night. But I'll wear it all the time except then, okay?"

"Oh man, man! Coach I can't believe this, I can't! And you're gonna piss in front of me and let me watch you get that jock strap all wet and then let me take it home, right? Can I do that? Hey man, if I bring a really big rubber with me tomorrow, will you put it on too, just for a minute or two, so I can take it home too. I just want it, knowing that you unrolled it on that enormous big dick that I just know you've got in there. Okay, can I?"

"Definitely man, definitely! Chris, tomorrow it is! Now, all we gotta do is keep a straight face if you're our server at the table tonight. What time do you go to work?"

"I go in at four, and start serving at four thirty. I'm in the main dining room, so if that's where you're eating, don't be shocked when you see me in my tight little waiter outfit. My pants are kinda tight. And Coach, please don't look down at my crotch, cause I know, when I see you again, I'm gonna subconsciously be smelling that hot crotch of yours, and I know damn well, it's gonna give me a big hard-on! I know it! That's what a hot looking and hot smelling man does to me, it does!"

––––––––––––

"Oh hey Coach, Hi! You been here long?"

"Hi Chris, no. I just got here a couple of minutes ago. Hey man, gotta tell you, you were real cool last night, during dinner. Nobody knew a damn thing! Well, yeah I did once. When you reached over me and put that strawberry desert down in front of me, I did happen to kinda glance down and saw what you meant about your dick getting out of control. I never thought about it yesterday, since everything happening was such a shock to me, but from what I noticed last night, for a white guy, you must have a pretty good dick on you, don't you?"

"Oh shit! Coach, was it showing that much last night? Was it showing? I kept trying to keep it hidden, but was it showing? But man, I knew, just knew you had that jock strap on that I got to smell, and even just being close to you and smelling you, that made me hard, real hard. You did have that jock strap on didn't you?"

"Yeah man, yes I did! You asked me to wear it, and I did! I had it on there at the table, and yeah, while you were kinda leaning over me, I knew I was kinda getting a little stiff some, and yeah man, I saw you were too!"

"Oh Coach, was it showing man, was it showing?"

"Well yeah, to me anyway! Hey Chris, I've never had any reason to look at some other guy's rod before, even any of my players, since I've never had any kind of a session with any of 'em like you and I had yesterday, so yeah, I noticed! Maybe today you'll show it to me so I can see how my sniffer guy is hung."

"Oh Coach, Coach! Oh shit man, shit! This talking is getting me so fucking hot, it is! Coach, just being around you is so fucking hot to me, I can't believe we're talking this way and doing this stuff together! Oh Coach, you are making me so fucking hot and horny! Did you wear that jock strap that you had on yesterday, and can I take it home with me?"

"Yeah, yeah I did, and I drank a lot of water too. You want me to piss in it before I take it off, right?"

"Oh shit yes! Oh Coach I can't believe you're gonna do this for me! I can't believe it! I've never had anybody else that's done this stuff for me like this. Thanks man, thanks!"

"Okay, come on. Let's move over this way a little more, get kinda hidden a little more, and get some more stuff between us and the path. Do many people know about this kinda hidden place back in here?"

"No, no. No Coach, I've never seen anybody else back in here, well 'cept for the guys I've brought back in here."

"So Chris, how many guys have you had back in here?"

"Oh Coach, I don't know! I found this place about three years ago, and so whenever it's nice enough out, and not fucking freezing, I've had some fun, probably three or four times a week. There's a lot of gay guys that visit this area, and once I can zero in on one of them, then I've got me some fun going. Seriously man, finding someone like you, a muscle built, marble statue, and a married one at that – I know I've never found another one like you! Your body is so fucking hot to me! You are so hot! That's why I want your 'pissed on jock strap' to take home with me, and then I'll be able to smell you whenever I can. I wanna get up in the mornings and put my nose in it! I wanna start my days and end my nights by smelling you, your crotch and your piss man! I wanna just be able to close my eyes and see you all over again, when I smell your smell! It smells so fucking sweet to me!"

"So Chris, what was the most outrageous thing that's happened to you up in here? What's happened?"

"Hey Coach, I don't have to tell you I'm gay, right? I mean, how often does a straight guy tell some hunk of a man that he wants to smell his crotch unless he's a gay, right?"

"Well yeah, I kinda guess maybe I figured that all out yesterday, specially when you told me to bring a jock strap for you and to be ready to piss for you. So yeah Chris, yeah, I figured that out!"

"Well anyway, one day, last summer, I met a guy that was staying in town at the hotel, and he and I were back in here, and he wanted to meet again the next day, so we did. What I didn't know was, almost his whole black gay softball team wanted to come with him, and all of his buddies wanted to use me too. He told them he was gonna fuck some white guy, up here along the trial, and they were all horny for some white ass, and so they all wanted to come, too. If you really wanna know what happened – I got fucked by eight big, thick, black, dicks that day! I and the original guy, we just started, and then one by one, they all kept coming, and when one guy was done, then the next one was standing there and ready. I gotta admit – that day was the wildest in here for me. I got gang banged that day, but I sure will never call it rape! Like they say, 'You can't rape the willing.' And I was willing! It was good man, really good! And one guy named Billy, his dick was so big and so thick – oh he felt so good!"

"Chris, were you okay after that? Where you okay?"

"Oh yeah Coach, I was okay! Tired, yeah! The only problem I really had was getting 'em to understand I had to go to work. The last couple of 'em, I really had to make 'em hurry up and do me – and my ass – fast. I had to get back to my place and get ready to get to work! But my biggest problem was, I wanted to get fucked by all of 'em, and not miss one or two. The day before, when the guy that had fucked me then, told me that he was gonna tell his buddies about me, he said that there would probably be eight guys coming up with him, and I told him that I wanted to get fucked by all of 'em. And I did! So I got fucked by him again, and – his eight buddies!"

"Uhh, Chris! I've never been fucked in the ass before, so I'm not sure just what it feels like or anything, but was your ass okay that night? I mean man, waiting tables takes a lot of walking. Were you okay?"

"Yeah, I was okay, but I will tell you, I needed to take some extra restroom visits to dump some of the cum shots they left up in me! My ass kinda dripped all night, and I had to make me an 'ass pad,' with some toilet paper, to keep it from dripping out. Other than that, nine guys in your ass in one day is fun, fucking fun – well for a gay guy, anyway! First and last time that's ever happened for me, but if I can ever get that set up again, I'll do it in a minute!"

"Oh Chris, Chris! I'd heard gay guys do, do some different stuff, but I sure as hell never heard of any guy getting fucked by nine different guys in one day! Shit man, I can't imagine that happening!"

"Hey, like I said, that was the only time! If it could happen again, especially with big, black, thick dicks like that team had, there is no way I'd stop it, if I could get it to happen again. But for right now, that was my only time. And talking about some fun stuff! You gonna let me watch you piss in that jock that I get to take home? I gotta see this!"

"Uhhhh, so like what am I supposed to do here guy? Take my shorts off and just pee on myself? I don't know what you want me to do."

"Hey man. Let me get all undressed, cause what I want you to do, is take your shorts off, and maybe your shoes so they don't get peed on, and keep the jock on. I want you to start peeing with the jock on, and after it's wet, then pull your dick out and pee the rest on me. Okay? That okay with you?"

"Hell man, I guess! Chris, I gotta tell you man, I ain't never done nothing even close to anything like this with any guy, so whatever turns you on, I guess it's okay with me. So far, everything's been okay, yeah – to me maybe a little crazy, but hey – we all need to do some different stuff once in a while, and I wanted some fun during this week, and I guess maybe this is it!"

Chris got fully stripped down, looked at Coach and said, "Well you wanted to see just what the little white guy was hanging, and so here it is! Not the biggest, but I gotta tell you, it shoots good!"

"Hey man, like I said, from what I kinda saw at the table last night, I thought it might be a little bigger than the normal, and I'd sure say from what I see, it is. It's fat too, ain't it?"

And as Coach was speaking, he was removing his running shorts and his shoes and socks as Chris had suggested, and was now standing there with only his jock strap on. Chris knelt down on his knees, right in front of the very big bulging crotch, and took a deep breath. "I wanna watch you pee Coach! I wanna watch you do it. Then spray it on me man, spray me. Let me smell your piss all over me please – please."

Standing there, and kinda shaking his head back and forth slightly as if to say, 'I cannot believe I am doing this,' Coach attempted to loosen his bladder so that the extra water he had been drinking, during his hike, would start flowing out. And knowing that warm water goes through the ole body faster, he had loaded up on some warmer water. As he stood there encouraging his body to cooperate, Chris stayed knelt in front of him, and as he licked his lips about four times, he stared at the bulge.

"There, there it comes Coach, it's peeing man, it's coming. Oh yeah man, it's getting that jock all wet! Oh yeah man, oh yeah!"

"Oh Coach can I pull your jock down? Can I do that? I wanna feel you pee on me man. Can I pull your jock down, please?"

"Yeah, yeah. Go ahead Chris, go ahead!"

With that 'okay,' Chris reached up, slid a finger in under the elastic waistband of the jock, and pulled it down. Not surprised, since Chris could obviously see that Coach had a major hard-on as he peed, Chris had to pull the jock strap way out, to get all of the Coach's cock out and free from the strap.

"Oh shit man! Oh man, look at that cock on you! Oh Coach, that is a fucking monster man, it is a fucking monster! Oh Coach it is beautiful! What a fucking cock!"

As Chris expounded on the beauty, and the enormous size of the coach's cock, he moved his face directly in front of the flow and allowed the warm yellow water to hit him all over his face, and then down into his throat. He stayed in place until Coach had finally emptied his bladder.

Now not saying anything, but taking his chances of being off base and maybe getting yelled at, and not asking for permission, but yet praying that what he was about to do was going to be okay, he reached up with his left hand, softly took a hold of the coach's cock, and aimed it for his mouth. He very silently listened for any comments of complaint. He heard none! Leaning slightly forward, he opened his mouth – as widely as possible – and allowed his mouth to slide over the thick black dick that he was rapidly falling in love with. Coach said nothing. He simply stood there in somewhat of a shock. He did not know that he was going to be getting his dick sucked on. He was watching his dick going into another man's mouth, and he had never had his dick inside of some man's mouth before. This had never happened before, and he never thought it ever would. He had not planned on this happening and he had never even wished to do this! But for some unknown reason, doing some of this stuff with Chris was making him do some very different and, to him, some very funny stuff. Stuff he had never thought about, but nothing that was making him want to stop, or to tell Chris, "No!" Things like – letting Chris suck on his cock! He did not know any of this was going to happen, he had not planned or tried to find anything like this – it was so truly out of the normal for him, and so far away from his usual being – but yet, he was not stopping it. Mentally he wondered if, and for what reason he was letting Chris take total control of everything, and yet he did not find any problem, with it? Mentally but silently, he told himself, "I'm the coach. I'm the one that is supposed to be in control and telling the others what to do, and how to do it. I'm totally out of place here. One of my "players" is controlling me – the coach – and everything that is happening with me. This is not right! This never happens! But, I really don't want to tell him to stop. What is with me, why am I doing this? I am actually enjoying it. Am I supposed to?"

Chris swallowed the first five inches, then reached up, placed his hands back on the coach's tight muscled hips, and at the same time, pulled the coach's torso forward, as he pushed his face forward, so that he could actually force the last five inches down, and into, the back of his throat. He chocked. He had all ten inches of cock in his mouth! All ten inches of one magnificently thick, muscular, and stiff cock! More than a mouth full – much more!

"You okay guy? You okay?" Coach asked as he slightly put his hands on the top of Chris's head.

Chris could not answer, but he did manage to shake his head up and down some, to let Coach know that he had heard the question, and was okay.

Chris was totally happy, but shocked that he was actually sucking on the coach's enormous dick, and without even asking first. His own ragging hard-on was evidence that he was living a dream. He had the coach in his mouth, and his own dick was standing as if in a parade. All of a sudden he felt the juices of his own dick let fly, and that feeling made him hump and bang the coach's cock as if he had never had a dick in his mouth before.

The coach grabbed onto Chris head, and in the fashion, normal to any male being, human or animal, he reacted to the excitement that Chris was pumping into this dick. A ten-inch long dick, stuck down into some guy's mouth, is definitely a mouth full, but Chris was taking it like a professional.

All of a sudden, Coach let out with a muttered, "Oh Chris, Chris, I'm gonna cum man, I'm gonna cum!"

Chris attempted a, "Yeah man yeah!" but with his mouth as full as it was, the words were more action, than words.

Just as quickly as Coach had given Chris the warning, it all broke loose. The coach let out with, "Oh man, oh man! Chris, I'm cummmin man, I'm cumin! Oh shit man I can feel it shooting out! Oh shit – oh shit! Oh what a feeling – what a feeling! Oh Chris, I just shot everything in you! Oh man, oh what a feeling!"

Chris now had a hell of a lot more than a mouth full. He attempted to swallow as fast as he could, but the coach just released way too much cum, way too fast, for Chris to manage taking all of it. He swallowed as much as he could, and half of it slid out the corners of his mouth and down onto the ground.

Slowly both men attempted to recover.

Coach actually stood there in somewhat of a state of shock realizing what had just happened. He had just been sucked off by a man for his very first time. In fact, that was the very first time that he had ever had his dick stuck in some man's mouth. He was not unhappy about what had happened, but he was shocked. When he started shooting off, that was his pinnacle of shock and joy! He did not know he was going to get sucked off, nor even let Chris take his cock in his mouth. Internally, he was glad that Chris had not asked if he could suck him off, because without a question for permission, Coach was not forced into making a decision, of saying "Yes or No." He was just very pleased that it had 'just happened,' with no statement of, "Yeah, it's okay – go for it," nor even a decline of permission. It just happened! And he was very quick to realize that what had just happened, was an experience and a feeling that he would never be able to duplicate! Attempting to regain his composure, and some lever of normal existence, he simply knew that what he had just felt and experienced, was a once in a lifetime experience.

Chris was in heaven, total heaven. He never thought that he had any chance of getting that dick to suck on, and when it happened, he was shocked, happy as hell, but none the less, shocked! He too was glad that it had 'just happened,' and that he did not need to ask for a 'sucking permission' statement.

Finally regaining some strength and some composure, Coach looked down at Chris, still knelling down right in front of his enormous dick, and asked, "You okay guy, you okay?

"Oh hell yes man, hell yes! Coach I never intended to do that and I sure as hell never thought I'd have been allowed to, but man alive, thank you – thank you! What a beautiful big dick you've got man! Man alive, what a dick! You asked me earlier what was the most exciting thing that I had ever done here, well – it just changed! Getting fucked by nine guys in one day was great, but Coach, taking that enormous big dick of yours and getting to eat your cream man, that was the tops! Seriously man, it was the tops!"

"You know Chris! I'm a coach. I've been around a lot of guys in the nude, and I've heard a lot of stuff about what gay guys do to each other, but I had never, until now, ever done anything with another guy. All I can say right now it, thank you man – one hell of a big thank you! I will admit, I've never told anybody, but I've often wondered just what it'd be like to have some guy suck my cum out of my dick, and now I know! I just know that from this time forward, if I hear, or maybe even overhear someone talking about getting a blow job from some guy, I'm gonna have to control my expression on my face, or I will be breaking out into one big, broad grin, just remembering this day. I sure didn't know any of this was gonna happen today either, but I sure don't have any bitches about it! And I never knew that having a climax, could ever feel anything like that! Thanks Chris, thanks for one unforgettable moment in life."

Looking up at the coach, Chris attempted a very big warm thank you back, but felt as if his 'thank you' was just not strong enough to really express his true feelings.

"Hey Coach, I brought that rubber with me that I mentioned yesterday. I bought an Extra Large size, and now I wonder if I can roll that on you? Your dick's got some cum and some piss on it, and I want to unroll that rubber on it, so that when I take it back off, that cum and that piss will be rolled up inside of it and I can smell it and lick it later – like after I jack off, just thinking about you and what you've let me do. Can I put that on you now?"

"Yeah, sure. Hell yes you can man. You sure can! You've got me into doing some stuff like I've never done before, so having you unroll a rubber on me right now sounds kind of fun."

Chris reached over to his shorts and took out the Extra Large Magnum condom, opened it, and put it on the tip of the coach's dick, and started to unroll it. Although the coach's dick had not yet gone fully soft, it had softened slightly, until, that is, when Chris started to handle it with the rubber, and rather moving the skin back and forth some. The action was definitely enough to where the coach now had another major, major hard-on.

"Oh shit man. Chris, I guess I'm just not used to having some guy handling my dick. I didn't expect it to react like that. Hey, just having you unroll that on me is feeling good, damn good! Hell it's been a long time since I've even had a rubber on, and I guess maybe I forgot how fucking good it feels to have one unrolled on my ole dick. Hey, I might have to go back to using condoms again, just to get that feeling. That feels good – damn good!"

Chris got the full length of the rubber unrolled and stretched out over the coach's cock, then put his mouth on it for a second, pushed it down into the back of his throat, and then after taking his mouth off of it, rolled it back up and sniffed it as he did. As he took it off of the coach's cock head, the coach did still have a very major and excited hard-on.

"Hey Chris, thanks for that! I'm glad you thought to do that! That was great! I guess maybe you do that to a lot of guys, right?"

"No, no I don't. I gotta admit, that is the first time that I have ever done that to some guy and his dick, but honestly man, yesterday when I saw this slab of steak sticking out here, it just got me so fucking horny that I just knew then, that I really wanted to do that, and I got that rubber last night, and put it in my pocket, so I'd make sure I didn't forget it today. Tonight, maybe after I feed you some good ole dining room food for supper, I'll take that rubber out, unroll part of it and have me one happy hell of a good time smelling you and licking some of your juices off of it. Hey Coach, while you're lying there in bed tonight with your wife, just remember that I'm in my own room there, on the edge of the lodge property, and I'm sniffing and licking on your rubber. She's got ahold of you, and I've got ahold of your slippery, smelly, rubber that you had on your stiff, hot, thick, beefy cock! Oh man, you don't know how I'd love to but another rubber on me, and then put my dick up in your ass so I could smell your ass juices on it too."

Still knelt down in front, Chris looked up at the coach and asked, "How in the hell am I ever gonna be able to serve you in the dining room tonight? I'm gonna take one look at you and melt, fucking totally melt!"

"Hey Chris! You think you got a problem! I'm gonna take one look at you and I'm gonna have a ragging hard-on that I'll never be able to hide. Make damn sure I'm seated at the table, with the tablecloth covering me before you come in the room. And Chris, tape that dick of yours down so it don't show. We sure don't want people asking us why we both have hard-ons showing during dinner."

"Hey Coach, know how I told you about those nine softball players using my ass? Is there any way you'll be the number ten please!!?? I know it's not the same day, and those guys are not here, but oh Coach, I'd love to know I've had you up in my ass, and do me just like those guys did to me."

"Hey, thank God you asked! Yeah man, yeah! I was kinda hoping and praying that you'd ask, cause I'm not sure when in the hell I'd ever get a chance to be with some good player like you, and I didn't want to just ask if I could fuck your tight ass or not, but thank goodness, now I know I can. Chris you are showing me some good fun stuff that I've never done before, and honestly man, when I shot off in your mouth, that was when I decided that I needed to follow through and get in your ass today too, or I knew I'd be having some trouble trying to keep my mouth closed and not say the wrong thing, or ask the wrong thing, sometime around my University guys. There is no way now, that I can go home and not know what that feels like too. You gonna be able to take it up in your ass without some lube? I don't wanna hurt you any."

"Oh Coach, yeah I'll manage, I gotta. It's already juicy with your cum on it, and I know I'll have to take it a little slower than usual, but Coach, hell yes I will get that up in there. I gotta have it!"

With that statement being said, Chris grabbed ahold of the trunk of a tree, leaned in toward it, spread his feet some, and softly stated, "Oh please fuck me – oh please fuck me."

Without any further talking, Coach grabbed ahold of his stiff rod, aimed it for Chris's ass, slowly moved in closer, grabbed Chris around the waist, then softly asked, "Ready," then gently started pushing the big black head, of his big black rod, into Chris's ass.

Chris slightly jerked as the mushroom head actually poked in. Not a gently nice sliding entry, but definitely much more of a 'poke and a pop,' which was necessary to get the large, thick, round mushroom head to spread Chris's ass enough to get it in.

As it popped in and found its interior space within Chris's hole, Chris did let out with a loud, "Oh my God, oh shit! Oh Coach, wait a minute! Oh man, oh that was like, oh man – oh yeah, oh – yeah, that hurt there for a second. Damn, I knew that dick head of yours was big from having it in my mouth, but damn, shit, I think it got bigger once it headed for my ass. Oh Coach. Hey, – I'm okay now – but I really felt it when it went in. Oh shit man – that did hurt there for a second, but Coach, I knew that was gonna happen when I asked to get fucked, so it sure as hell is not your fault. That baby really got my ass opened, and opened good! Now, you're up in there, fuck the hell out of me. Think of one of your hottest built, muscled, athletic football players back home, visualize his ass running across the field, and make believe you are in that ass, and do it! Fuck me man, fuck me – and make believe you are fucking your hot assed football stars in the ass!"

"Chis, Chris, you sure you're okay? You sure you want me poking you back here? You okay? Seriously, I did not mean to hurt you, and I don't want to hurt you anymore man, I don't!"

As Chris stood there with his arms outstretched and grabbing onto the tree, and his ass pushed back toward the coach as if to be begging for some action back there, Chris answered, "I am perfectly okay. Honestly man, I am okay. You just gotta know that when a dick head that big goes up in you, you are gonna feel it. It feels like you just pushed a full sized grapefruit up in there, but Coach, a guy's gotta do that if he expects to get the feelings that I've got up inside of me now. Now, I am in heaven, one very good heaven. Use me. Fuck me like you've never been able to fuck before. It's up in there, and I want the rest of it up in there too. Push it in man, push it in so that I know I've got all of you up in there. Then, pound the hell out of me. Don't miss maybe your only chance in life, to pound the hell out of some guy's ass. I'm asking for it, go to it!"

And he did! The coach heard Chris's instructions to pound the hell out of his ass, and although it did take him a few minutes of going slow, going soft, and going gentle, Chris did manage to convince him to pound his ass and to use his ass like he had never been able to do before. Chris moved up, right against the tree with his chest and his gut on the tree, his feet spread to the left and to the right of the trunk, and his arms wrapped around the tree, actually hugging it, while he again begged the coach to pound his ass. Chris finally did manage to convince the coach that this was his chance, and it could be his only chance, to use some guy's ass like jumping on a springboard. He told the coach, "Let me feel all of you and your hot body pounding on me and in me! I want all of you!"

After some very good, ten minutes or so of some 'big, black, stiff, thick, dick in a tight, small, white, asshole, all of a sudden, the coach let out with an almost yell, that he had to cum. "Oh my God Chris, Chris, I gotta cum again! Chris, I gotta cum! I didn't think I'd have to cum again, but I gotta. I gotta cum!"

As quickly as he could, Chris responded with a very enthusiastic, "Good! Do it, do it! Shoot in me Coach – shoot in me!" And then almost immediately he continued, "Oh yeah man, oh yeah! Oh that is so fucking warm up in there! Oh Coach, shoot man, keep shooting! Fill me man, fill it! Oh Coach, thank you man, thank you! Oh, I have not been fucked like that for one hell of a long time! Oh thanks! Thank you! Oh God that felt good!"

Chris unwrapped his arms from around the tree, and just as Coach pulled his still stiff and hard boner back out of Chris's ass, Chris immediately spun around, knelt down onto his knees and sucked both of the coach's balls into his mouth!"

"Oh wow, oh shit man, oh man that feels good! Oh Chris, I sure did not expect that, but thanks man, thanks! I've never had my nuts sucked on before, but I sure do love the way that feels. God man – that is great! Thanks!"

And as Coach uttered his last "Thanks," Chris pulled off, letting first the left ball to slide out, and then the right ball to follow suit. Coach looked down, grabbed Chris under the armpits, helped him stand up, and asked, "Hey Chris. You made that comment about wishing you could stick your dick up in my ass so that you could take home some of my ass juices, right?"

With a very puzzled look on his face, Chris answered, "Yeah?"

Coach answered, "You got another rubber with you?"

"Yeah, yes I do! Why? Coach what are you saying? Coach can I? Is that what you're saying?"

"Yeah, I think so Chris, I think so. Chris, you've taught me so much stuff yesterday and today, stuff that just maybe I've kinda wondered about, and yes, even heard some of the college boys talking about – usually when I'm not supposed to be listening – that right now, I think maybe I need to know, by actual experience, just what it is like to get a dick stuck up in my ass, and honestly, if it's not with you, then I'm never gonna find out. Do you think I can take your dick? I know I've got a really fat dick, and you really felt it when I poked it up in you, so do you think maybe I can take yours without too much bad pain. I can take some pain, and I know already it is gonna hurt – I already know that – but I guess maybe I'm just curious enough to take the pain, so I can have that experience, too. You got another rubber?"

"Oh yeah man, yes I do! I brought two, just in case something happened to one of 'em, so yeah I've got one. Oh

Coach – my God man – I never, in my greatest dreams, ever thought that this could happen."

As Chris grabbed the second rubber out of his shorts pocket, he said, "Here! Here it is! Coach – Coach you wanna unroll it on me like I did to you?"

"Yeah, yeah I do. Good idea man, good thinking."

The coach did open the package, and did unroll it onto Chris's dick, saying as he did, "Hey! This is one of the Extra Large Magnums too, isn't it? You are pretty well filling this baby up, so I guess maybe your dick is kinda on the larger size too then, ain't it?"

"Yeah, I guess." Chris answered. "See that's the size I keep on hand all of the time, since I only like to play with the really big dick guys, like you, and it might be a little too big for my rod, but at least I fill enough of it to where it doesn't come off. I do admit, I cannot unroll a regular sized rubber on my dick. When I first got one I thought I did not know how to unroll it since I could not get it to unroll. Then a friend pointed out to me, that my dick was too thick to get it on, and then he gave me a large sized one, and it fit."

"Okay, it's on. Now, I'm gonna lean up against that tree that you leaned on, and all I can ask of you is, please do go slow! Please remember, I have never had anything stuck up in my ass before, and that is the whole reason for what we are doing today! Slow and easy, okay!? I just wanna know before this trip is over, that yes, I also got a dick pushed up in my ass."

As Chris leaned over slightly, he spit some mouth saliva onto his dick, slid it around some and especially up toward the tip, and very slowly and very carefully, moved in toward the coach's hot looking tight ass hole.

Carefully he moved forward, aimed his dick at the coach's hole, found the opening, grabbed the coach around the waist, and slowly started in. He felt the coach rather jerk some, but not much, and he made no bad sounds. Another inch in, and he did hear the coach make a very welcoming accepting sound. Then he did hear him utter, "Yes, oh yes. Oh yeah Chris, I feel you up in there! Yeah, I feel you. You in very far?"

"No Coach, no. Just the tip. You wanting more?"

"Oh hell yes man, hell yes! Oh man, give it to me, give it to me. Oh yeah push, push! Oh Chris, I had no idea getting fucked in the ass like this felt so fucking good! Oh yeah, yeah Chris, you're in. I can tell – I can feel it up in there! Do me man, do me! Yeah, pound me like you told me to pound you! Yeah, oh hell yeah! Oh my God man, I've never felt anything like this before – oh shit man, that feels good! Oh Chris, you doing okay man – you doing okay?"

"Oh hell yes Coach, hell yes! I never, in a thousand years, thought that I'd ever get a chance like this! Oh coach – damn I wish I was one of your football players! Man, could I be a player for you! I'd be making you coach me every fucking night in the locker room! Oh man, your ass feels so good to me. Oh man, I'm getting close to cummin already man – I'm getting close Coach – I'm getting close! Oh Coach, oh man – I'm gonnnna cum – I'm gonnnnna cum! I've gotta cummmmm–!"

"Oh Chris, I can feel that! I know it's all in your rubber, but I could feel you letting loose. Oh hell, now I wish you didn't have that damn rubber on. Oh, I would have loved to have felt that cream hitting the edges of my ass! Oh Chris, I've been fucked! Now I've been fucked! Never in my wildest dreams did I think I would ever get it in the ass, let alone this week-end, but man, I just did, and I am damn glad I did."

After resting up against the hot muscled back of the coach, Chris pulled out, put his hands on the coach's butt cheeks, stooped down, pulled the cheeks apart, and immediately threw his face in the coach's butt crevasse and threw his tongue into the coach's ass hole. He pushed his tongue in as far as he could, then licked around as much as he could before pulling back out and licking the outer edges, where he could have some better tongue action."

"Oh Chris, oh Chris! Oh man, I never thought of this! I never even thought that maybe I could ask you to do that! Oh man, you are licking chewing and eating on my ass, oh I love it. Chris, kiss my ass! I mean really kiss my ass. Oh lick my ass and clean it up good and sweet! Clean my ass, let me feel it back there! When this is done, I wanna be able to really say, I've had my ass kissed. And I do mean, really, really kissed! Kissed by one hot, hot, hot stud of a guy! This is gonna be days to remember, believe me!"

As Chris pulled his face back, Coach turned around, put his hands under Chris's armpits, pulled him up and said, "Chris, I have no idea of how I can thank you for what has happened. These few days, were supposed to be somewhat of a vacation for me and my wife, but I will tell you that it has become a very important educational experience for me, instead. Back at the university, there are a lot of meetings and conversations about students, and especially athletes and the different life styles that they have – well in other words, the gay students – and I will admit that up until this time, I really have not been very much involved, nor cared too much, about what was being discussed. But Chris, you have now changed that for me. Of course I'm not gonna be able to tell people why I'm more interested in the conversations now, but this experience has shown me some new ways and new things, and has given me a new view on how to see other people, and what they do and how they live. Damn, I'm glad you love to smell old hot and sweaty crotches. I've never had a man want to do that with me, but I sure am glad you did, and I'm even more glad that I let you do it, instead of taking my

ole normal attitude that, 'That's sick!' Maybe rather on the weird
side when you first think of it, but hey, weirder things do happen.
Thanks Chris! I'm gonna be looking at all of the students, and
especially my football players, under a different light, and from
what I just learned, I just might want to get back in touch with a
former coach that we got rid of a couple of years ago. We got rid
of a wrestling coach, and I know, I was just as involved in talking
about his 'life style' as everybody else was, but thank goodness,
he's not too far away. And I know how to get in touch with him,
cause I think the time has now come, for me to apologize to him,
face to face, for any bad comments that I might have made about
him, if he ever heard them or not! I'm gonna ask him if there is
a way, 'someway,' that I can make that up to him. I'll let him tell
me what I can do – and with that body on him – I will agree to
anything. I may just have to mention this particular trip and how
much I learned, just to make sure he is really in step of just why I
am now apologizing – for anything that I might have said."

———————————

"Ladies and Gentlemen, I know that tonight will be your
last night here for dinner, and I'd certainly like to let you all know
that you have certainly been a very enjoyable table of guests to
wait on, and to do things for – each and everyone of you! We as
staff, do attempt to do something a little extra for each of you,
whenever we can. I hope you do remember your visit here at the
lodge as maybe one that was very educational and very enjoyable.
I certainly do know that I will be remembering each one of you in
a very special way, too. Waiting on each of you has been special
for me, and we do try to do whatever is necessary to make your
visit with us extra special. I do hope I have managed to do that for

each of you. Thank you for visiting with us, and I do hope all of you have had some very new, special, educational and enjoyable, unexpected experiences while here, and I do hope they have been days, and events, for each of you to remember for ages. And as they say, 'Do remember to stop and smell the roses – or whatever there is close by.'"

And as he glanced around the table and rather toward, but not directly at the coach – casually holding his silver serving tray down in front of his waist <u>and his crotch area</u> – he tipped his head in a rather royal manner, and added, "And if there is anything additional that I can do for any of you, do please let me know. I hope your visit has been great, and outstanding! Thank you for being here, and if you can, do please, please – come again!"

About the Author

Wade Wright is an older gay man, now partly, or fully retired, *depending on the circumstances at the time*, living in Arizona as he has for the past fifty years. Grandfather of four, and the survivor of two sadly shortened gay relationships!

Wade Wright is also the author of:

- ***Family Matters: And Sometimes, It Just Does Not Matter***
- ***Totally Unexpected***
- ***The Carpet Installer***
- ***Jay, Jake and Jimmy***
- ***In Cemetery Park***
- ***Marshmallow Cream – And Some Hard Pieces of Chocolate***
- ***"Yes Cops Do It, - Oh Yeah!"***
- ***The Two Straight Guys***

- Apartment 117
- Married Men On The Loose
- We Have Just Landed – Vol. 1 and Vol. 2

All Available from Amazon.com,
The NazcaPlainsCorp.com, or your local bookstore.